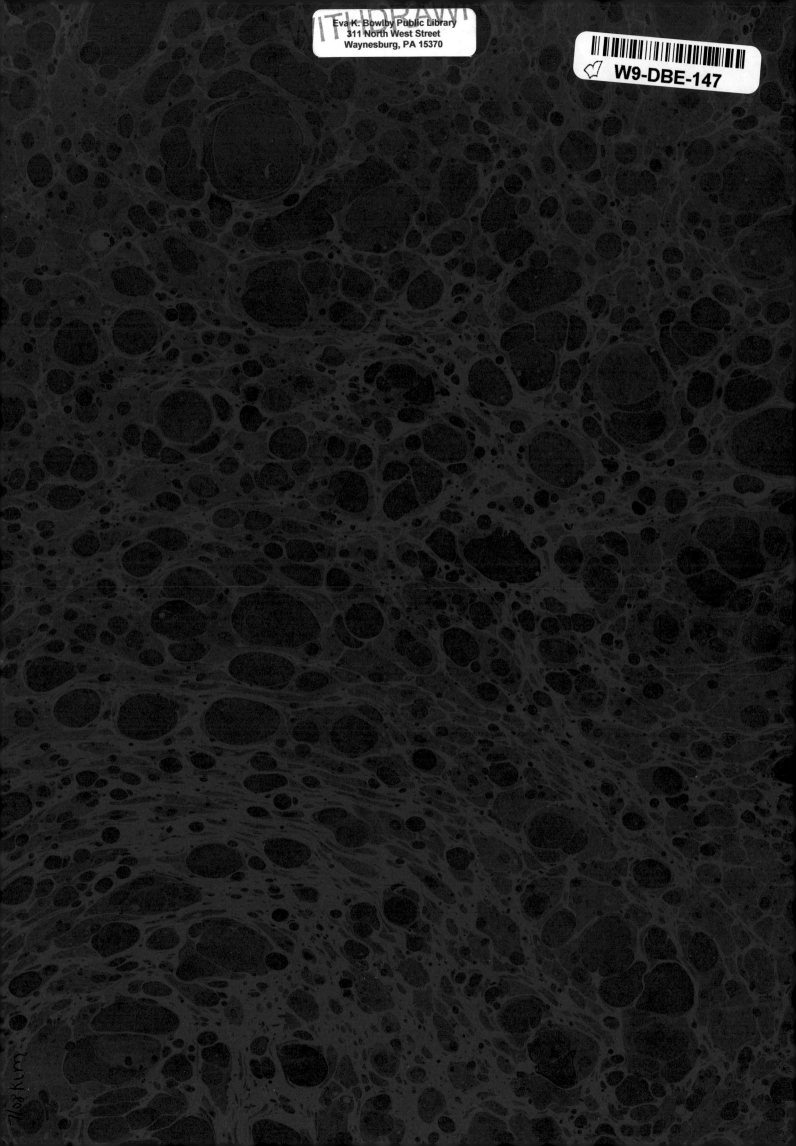

The Enchanted World

CALES OF CERROR

The Enchanted World

TALES OF TERROR

by the Editors of Time-Life Books

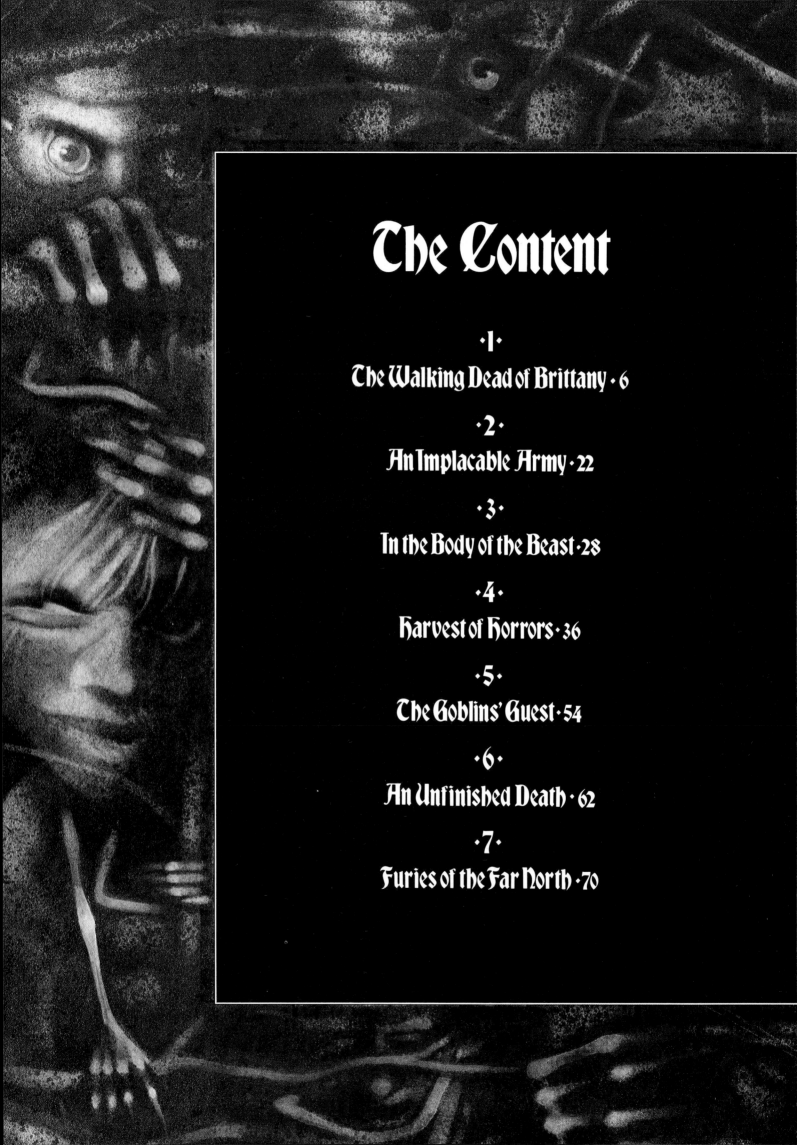

The Content

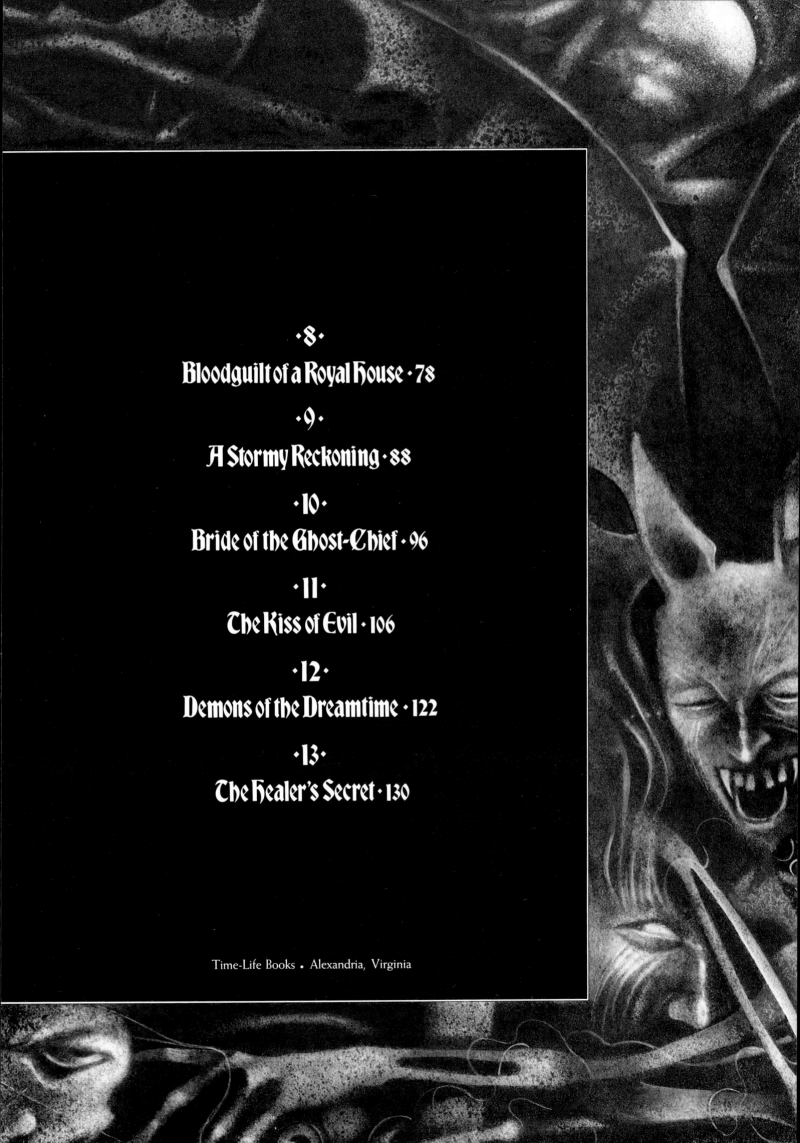

Time-Life Books • Alexandria, Virginia

·1·
The Walking Dead of Brittany

In Brittany, the living knew they did not dwell alone. Tall stones set in rings or rows by unnamed ancients stood guard over a landscape filled with secrets. On the tidal islands shrouded by sea fogs, the cart of the Ankou—the name Bretons gave to Death himself—rattled across the causeways at night, heavy with its invisible cargo. High on the barren moors, or in the forested hinterland of the Argoat, ghosts walked on mysterious errands, completing the unfinished business of lives cut short.

The border between the worlds of light and shadow was, paradoxically, hard to find but easily crossed. It was sometimes said that only a person doomed to die before the year's end could see the forms of those who had gone before. But conversations between dead and living were neither unknown nor forbidden. The spirits of the departed often accosted those whose hearts still beat, to tell a doleful story or enlist their aid.

Obligations between friends or kinfolk did not end when the mourners filed out of the churchyard. In the kitchens of houses that the Ankou had visited, a bowl of milk and a platter of crepes stood ready to entertain the homesick spirit of the deceased. Debts had to be paid, and promises made before death were still to be honored. If such vows were breached, those who reneged should be prepared to suffer the consequences. There were many tales, handed down in the old language, to remind them of the risks.

One story concerned a pair of devoted friends named Philip and Cado, young men of a moorland parish. They had passed their childhoods in each other's company, learning to hunt and fish, filching apples in tandem, struggling together at their lessons. Inseparable even when they grew to manhood, they swore that whoever married first would have the other as his best man. In time, both fell in love with the same young woman. To the bemusement of their neighbors, the pair courted her together without apparent jealousy or rancor. But their beloved Marguerite was wiser than her suitors; she knew that sooner or later a choice would have to be made.

On the day Marguerite arrived at her decision, Philip was away from home. He

Two Breton peasants, friends since boyhood, courted the same young woman. No acrimonious word nor jealous gesture passed between them, but the love triangle ended in horror.

had done what no other man in the village would do; he had agreed to stand as godparent to the fatherless child of a poor, half-witted peasant girl. Setting tongues wagging, Philip escorted the sickly babe and its shamefaced mother to the parish church in a nearby market town. He announced to all and sundry that no child, whatever its parentage, should be denied the hope of heaven. The baptism came none too soon. Safely christened, the ailing infant fell into a fit and died on the way back to the village.

When Philip returned that night, his mother poured him out a cup of cider and said that his friend Cado had come to call, looking pale and haggard. She passed on Cado's message: He needed to see Philip urgently, and begged him to come at sunrise to the tall cross up on the moor, where two paths met.

Only the baker was awake in the village when the young man set out for the rendezvous. Philip could smell the day's first loaves browning in the oven. As he climbed the gorse-covered moor, he was puzzled by a faint tapping sound, as if someone were knocking on a door. But there was no habitation nearby, not even a shepherd's hut. When he reached the meeting-place, the mystery was solved. The lavender light of morning revealed a long, forked shape, swinging from the arm of the cross, its feet tapping gently against the wooden upright.

Cado, sightless eyes bulging, blackened tongue protruding, was there before him. Philip's scream of anguish resounded off the hills, and its echo pursued him back to the village. Sobbing, he ran first to break the news to Marguerite. He stood silently by while she tore her hair, scratched at her face and nearly choked with uncontrollable weeping.

"So Cado was the one you loved," he said. But Marguerite's mother, who had been sitting smoking her pipe by the hearth, rose up to tell him it was not as it seemed. Only yesterday, she said, Marguerite had told Cado that Philip was her chosen mate. Then Philip understood what had happened and why.

The two lovers grieved for their friend, but they saw no reason to delay their marriage. They agreed that there would be no dancing at the feast, as a mark of respect for their departed companion. Then they threw themselves into plans and preparations, and banished all thoughts of the suicide's body, now rotting—as custom decreed—on the gibbet of his own devising.

It came time for the prospective bridegroom to tour the countryside, issuing the wedding invitations to his neighbors, friends and kinfolk. As he rode with another young man across the moor, he spoke of the promise, made years before, that only Cado should be his groomsman when he wed. He would not rest easily, he said, if the vow was not honored, at least by a gesture. Leaving his friend to hold the horses, Philip climbed the long slope to the cross that was now a gallows.

At his approach, a flock of fat crows flew off the decaying thing that dangled there. Cap in hand, Philip came closer. He spoke up to remind his old friend of

*On the high moor where two paths met, a suicide's corpse hung from
a cross, a mute reproach to the friend who had been luckier in love.*

the promise, and told Cado that the place of best man awaited him at the nuptial feast. Then, conscience salved, he went away to speak his words of invitation to warmer ears elsewhere. As he hurried down the slope, he heard a flapping of wings and looked back to see the birds descending once again to their banquet.

When the day of the wedding arrived, guests came from all over the district, the women in their best lace caps and fichus, the men with their silver buttons polished. Cider flowed, cool and golden, for the drinking of toasts, moving even the plainest-spoken farmhand to lyrical flights in praise of the happy couple. Philip, one arm clasped around his beloved Marguerite, lifted his cup to reply in kind. Then a voice, coarse and mocking as a raven's, croaked out, "I must drink to my best beloved friend."

There in the doorway stood Cado, or what was left of him. The guests froze. The cup dropped from Philip's hand.

The specter lurched toward the bride and groom. "Where is my seat? You said you would keep a place of honor for me." The only reply was a stricken silence.

Again the ghost of Cado began to speak. With a creaking bow, he turned and asked the bride to dance. Marguerite's face blanched whiter than her ghostly suitor's bones, but her husband spoke up on her behalf. He explained that there was to be no dancing at this wedding feast, as a mark of respect for Cado's memory. A wheezing, clattering parody of laughter erupted from the spec-

ter's throat. The creature came closer and leaned across the table, its rank breath polluting the cider in the cups. Then it reached out to Marguerite and announced its intention to kiss the bride.

For the first time in his life, Philip raised an angry fist to his old friend, but the blow fell on empty air. Then he felt a prickling on the back of his neck and heard a sibilant whisper in his ear. It warned him that if he did not wish to see the wedding spoiled utterly, and the marriage too, he had better meet Cado at midnight, at the cross on the moor, to make amends. Then the unwelcome guest was gone.

The other members of the party made a few half-hearted efforts to rekindle the festive spirit, but it was clear that the groom's thoughts, and the bride's as well, were elsewhere. The couple withdrew for a hasty, private conversation and agreed that it would be dangerous for Philip to ignore Cado's request. Unplacated, his ghost could blight their lives in ways too hideous to think of. Soon thereafter, the guests made their excuses and departed from the hostelry, leaving the innkeeper shaking his head over platters of food uneaten and cider barrels unbreached. It would all, he reminded Philip, have to be paid for.

Philip brought Marguerite to the cottage he had furnished for her. Then, with many regrets, he left her there to pray for his safe return. His last sight of his new bride was a glimpse through a candlelit window of Marguerite removing her tall, lace wedding headdress; there passed through his mind the vision of her

replacing it all too soon with the dull brown cap traditionally worn by widows. He shuddered at the thought, but he had made his promise to Cado. Nothing would prevent him from fulfilling his vow and climbing to the cross on the high moor to make an end of the matter.

Guided by moonlight, Philip approached the hill where the cross bore its creaking burden. But as he set foot on the slope, he heard someone hailing him by name. A knight in white armor rode toward him. Philip waited, puzzled, for he knew no one sufficiently highborn to wear such apparel or own such a mount. Indeed, he had never seen an armored knight before, except in the parish churchyard, carved on the high stone calvary of saints and heroes. The horseman saluted him. Philip responded with a courteous greeting, but apologized for not recognizing someone who seemed nevertheless to be acquainted with him. The knight laughed, but did not lift his visor. He said that he knew Philip—and where he was heading at this dangerous hour. He offered to carry Philip up to the cross on horseback.

Bemused, but sensing the knight was, in some way, an ally, Philip climbed up behind him. On this night of menace, he would take without question any help that was offered. As the horse bounded up the slope, Philip clasped the knight around the waist to steady himself. The white armor was warm to the touch.

They pulled up a little way from the place where the outline of the cross stood stark against the sky, and a bundle of bones could be seen swaying gently in the breeze. As Philip dismounted, the knight instructed him to approach the skeleton without hesitation, clasp its right foot, or what remained of it, with his right hand, and announce that he had come to learn what Cado wanted of him. Philip did as he was bidden, steeling himself to clasp the skeletal foot. He could feel the dents where it had been pecked and pitted by the crows. Then he asked Cado what he desired of him. The skeleton kicked out violently, sending Philip flying, and the bones began to lurch about, as if battered by a storm. Then there came a groan, not from the thing hanging on the gibbet, but from the ground beneath it. It was Cado's voice, much distorted, yet it offered curses and imprecations that Philip had never heard pass his comrade's lips in life. It roared abuse at the mysterious

Rank with the stench of his own dead flesh, an unexpected guest
arrived late at the wedding. Approaching the bridal couple, the
revenant demanded one last kiss from the woman who had rejected him.

knight, whose intervention had deprived it of its rightful prey. Without his help, the bridegroom's bones, and not Cado's, would now be swinging from the cross, and the fair Marguerite would find a very different husband in her bed.

Philip ran back to the knight, who seemed indifferent to the rain of curses. There was, he said, nothing more Cado could do to Philip, and certainly nothing Cado could do to him. He pulled Philip up behind him, and the horse sped down the hill. When they had reached the bottom, Philip dismounted and thanked the stranger effusively. The knight raised a gauntleted hand to silence him. He was, he said, returning a favor. He reminded Philip of the dying child that he had taken to the baptismal font. Through that small act of kindness, a soul had been saved and elevated to the army of angels. He lifted his visor to reveal a countenance flooded with unearthly light, then he pressed his spurs into his horse's flanks and disappeared.

It was not only upon former friends that the dead made claims. A ghost in need might throw itself upon the mercy of any who still walked among the living.

One such encounter took place along the rocky north Breton coast. It happened upon a December night, in the bitterest winter ever known in that region. The tale concerned an old woman named Marie-Job, who made her living as a wagoner, but made her name as a witch. It was whispered that she knew the secret arts, had the gift of sniffing danger in the wind, and spun curses as deftly as her neighbors spun wool.

For such a woman, night held few terrors. When other folk huddled by firesides or stirred restlessly through bad dreams in their beds, Marie-Job was out with her aged horse, Mogis, driving a battered cart along the causeway that linked her island with the mainland. The coast was the haunt of wreckers and smugglers, who thought nothing of killing anyone who chanced upon them at work. But these evildoers were far more frightened of Marie-Job than she was of them. It was said that her old wagon, laden with goods from the market at Lannion, resembled that of the Ankou when it juddered out of the evening mists with its burden of newly harvested souls.

Formidable she may have been, but Marie-Job was fair to all and generous to her friends. If she had not been so, the terrible events of that long ago winter's night might never have taken place.

It was her custom, every Thursday in her life, to travel to the mainland to collect the new stock for the woman who ran the village shop. But in that particular December week, the weather was so bitter that Marie-Job considered abandoning her trip. Even the dead were affected, after a fashion: The cold cracked the tombstones in the cemetery and froze the ground so hard that no new corpses could be buried. Marie-Job announced that while she herself could endure the journey, she feared it would be too much for her poor old Mogis.

When the shopkeeper heard this, she came to Marie-Job in a panic. Friday was

the day the island quarrymen were paid for their labors. By noon, there would be two hundred of them storming into her shop, demanding fresh provisions and enough strong cider to drink away their silver and their troubles. The shopkeeper was counting on Marie-Job to bring fresh supplies from the Thursday market, for these quarrymen were as hard as the rocks they hammered, and if she could not sell them whatever they demanded, they would think nothing of raising fists huge as hams and boots hard as boulders, to vent their disappointments on her shelves and her shopboards. Marie-Job told her to dry her tears. Pulling on her shawl and mittens, she went off to the stable to harness Mogis, saying only that she knew she was a fool for doing this, for there was a smell of something wicked on the wind.

The journey to the mainland was colder than any Marie-Job remembered, but uneventful. She stabled Mogis in the inn yard, made her purchases, and returned to the hostelry at sunset for her customary supper of bread and soup before setting off home. The mistress of the inn was appalled that anyone should travel in such weather. She urged Marie-Job to stay the night, and even went so far as to offer a bed free of charge.

But Marie-Job refused. She liked, she said, to do things her own way. It was her habit to travel back from the market by night and give Mogis his breakfast oats in his own stable. The hostess urged her to think of the horse's well-being, if not her own. She told tales of beasts whose ears had snapped off in the cold and whose hooves had frozen to the cobblestones.

Marie-Job would not change her mind. She asked for a cup of hot coffee with a dash of brandy to warm her bones, then hitched Mogis to the wagon. But before she drove out of the inn yard, she confessed to the hostess that a little voice in her left ear had warned her to expect a hard trip home. The sooner it was over, said Marie-Job, the better.

Mogis knew the road home as well as his mistress, and needed no urging to trot as fast as the wagon would allow. Marie-Job tried to stay awake by counting the icy points of stars that pricked the sky. But soon her mind grew as numb as her body. Suddenly, she was jolted awake and nearly fell from the cart: Mogis had shied and stopped dead.

The road ahead was empty. Marie-Job flicked her whip over Mogis' bony flanks but the horse remained immovable, ears flattened back against his head. Marie-Job climbed down to find out what stood in the path. Peering into the darkness, she saw nothing. The barrier blocking the path was not of the visible world.

The witch-light glowed in Marie-Job's eyes as she traced the sign of the cross on the road with her whip handle. She uttered words of power, commanding the unseen entity to declare itself. From the roadside ditch a thin voice responded. Marie-Job found a small, wizened old man crouching there. She helped him up and he stood trembling, looking down at the road, his back bent nearly double.

What had he done, she demanded, to terrify her horse? He replied that it was not what he had done but what he carried that alarmed the animal. His burden, he explained, was nothing that the naked eye could see, but her horse knew what it was and would not move while it was anywhere on the road, before or behind.

Marie-Job thought quickly, then announced that she was not prepared to linger there all night, so the old man had better climb up into her cart and bring his invisible baggage along with him. That would at least allow Mogis to move on. The stranger accepted with alacrity, saying only that he was allowed to accept help but forbidden to ask for it.

It took all of Marie-Job's strength, and she was no slender slip of a maiden, to shove him into the cart. When he settled himself beside her, she could feel the axle bend. The planks creaked and groaned as if some huge load had been placed on the wagon. Yet her new companion was barely the size of a half-grown child and looked as if a good puff of wind would blow him away. She flicked the whip and Mogis moved on.

Marie-Job asked the old man if he was bound for the island. It was an idle question, merely to break the silence, for that road led nowhere else. "I am going where you are going," was the reply.

As they crossed the causeway onto the isle, she could see that Mogis was straining and sweating. When they reached the place where the road divided, Marie-Job asked her passenger where he wished to go. The answer came: the cemetery.

Marie-Job began to protest—only a madman would visit there at this hour, and anyway, the gates were locked at night. But her horse set off, of his own volition, down the cemetery track. The gate to the graveyard stood open.

"You see, we are expected," said the old man. And, as if his invisible burden had dropped away, he leaped lightly to the ground. Marie-Job picked up the reins and uttered a hasty command.

"Stay!" said the stranger, and Mogis refused to budge, no matter how hard his mistress urged him. Marie-Job muttered every spell she could think of, and made magic passes with her whip handle, but it was all for nothing. The old man explained that because she had offered help of her own free will, they were now in this together. If she tried to leave before time, the weight he had carried would fall on her shoulders. But, he reassured her, their work was almost done.

He named an island family, the Pasquiou, and asked to be taken to the plot where its members lay buried. It was easy to oblige, for only six weeks before, Marie-Job had attended the funeral of the last person to bear the name. She led the way, and the little man followed, groaning under his burden once again. She stopped at the tomb. He prostrated himself at its foot.

Then, in the moonlight, Marie-Job saw something that made her think she was dreaming. The slab of stone that covered the grave turned on its side, and the earth opened like a box. She reeled back from the stench of decay and heard something heavy thud into the pit. Trembling, she hastily crossed herself

On the bitterest night of a brutal winter, the wagon-driver Marie-Job
offered a ride to a traveler in distress. But this was no ordinary
passenger, and his face remained hidden all the long way home.

and gasped out a blessing on the souls of the dead. Helping souls, whispered the old man into her ear, was what this was all about. Marie-Job turned to find him standing upright. For the first time, his face was clearly visible. But where eyes should have been, there were only empty sockets, and an oblong crater was all that remained of the nose.

He called Marie-Job by name, although she had never given it, and urged her not to be frightened, for he had a story to tell that would make everything clear. He named a long-ago battle in the great wars that rocked France in Marie-Job's grandfather's time, and he spoke of two young soldiers, inseparable friends. One, Patrice Pasquiou, was mortally wounded. The dying man gave his comrade all the money he carried and asked him to swear a solemn oath. He wished his friend to buy him a burial in a grave that would be well marked and easy to find. When the war was over, the companion was to return, take up Patrice's bones and bury them on the Breton island where his ancestors lay.

The vow was duly made, but never kept. The dead man was buried with a score of other comrades in a shared and unmarked grave. At the war's end, the soldier started a new life, far away. He purchased a farm and raised a family. He prospered, aged, and finally died in his bed. But no sooner was he cold in his grave than some unseen power thrust him out of it. He would never be permitted to rest until he had fulfilled the long-

forgotten obligation. He was to retrieve Patrice's body from its unmarked mass grave and carry it, muffled in invisibility, to its proper resting-place.

As punishment for breaking his promise, the pilgrimage was made especially arduous. He could only move between midnight and cockcrow, and on every second night he was forced to walk backward, thereby losing three-quarters of the distance he had gained. His journey had so far taken nearly twenty years, and it might have lasted for another five if Marie-Job had not obliged him. So, as a gesture of appreciation, he would reveal a secret: It was time for her to wind up her affairs on earth.

"We will meet again soon," he said, and sank into the open grave.

Marie-Job stood stiff and rigid, perhaps from terror, perhaps from the frost eating into her bones. She turned back to her horse and saw that the sweat on his flanks had frozen into a hard, brittle glaze. Too weak to climb back into the wagon again, she clutched the halter and slowly led old Mogis home.

The next morning, the village shopkeeper went to Marie-Job's house to fetch the supplies she had ordered. She found her friend in bed, her face pinched and her breath halting. Marie-Job gasped out her story, and asked for a priest and a lawyer to be sent to her. Once she was satisfied that her material and spiritual affairs were properly disposed, she departed, to join her passenger of the night before. But she did not go alone, for on that very same day, her neighbors found her old horse Mogis dead in the stable.

His gruesome tale recounted, the stranger
sank down into the grave that gaped for him.

·2·

An Implacable Army

When harvests failed in medieval Germany, the specter of famine stalked the land, gathering up children, the old and the frail in its bony grip. Animals too went hungry, and vast armies of rats, driven from the empty granaries, scoured the countryside in their search for food.

In the usually rich fiefdoms of the Rhine Valley, one winter surpassed all others in the horrors it spawned. The summer had been hot and bright, and by late July the wheatstalks were bending under the weight of the ripening ears they bore. Then, less than a month before harvest, rainstorms swept through the golden valleys, beating down the crop and leaving the wheat smashed and rotting on the sodden ground. Soon the shadow of hunger lay over the land.

The famine was at its worst in the ancient town of Bingen, on the banks of the River Rhine. In their desperation, its townspeople turned their thoughts to their one hope of salvation: the well-stocked storehouses of their overlord, the wealthy and avaricious Bishop Hatto of Mainz. Surely, they reasoned, he could not continue to hoard his grain when starvation threatened his people?

For a week or more the Bishop made no reply to all their appeals for assistance. Then one morning a herald appeared with a message. Let those who were hungry and had not the means to pay for their grain, he said, assemble in the Bishop's great barn that afternoon. There they would get their just desserts.

When the appointed time arrived, an emaciated crowd had gathered outside the storehouse. Stony-faced attendants stood waiting, and at a signal they threw open the heavy timber doors. Immediately the crowd surged in. But they did not find wheat. There was nothing but a little chaff, stirred by the wind that sighed through the cracks in the wall. A growl of disappointment spread through the barn. Then everything went black. The great doors had swung shut.

Now anger turned to fear. Those who were near the doors tried to force them open, but they had been firmly secured. A child started wailing in the darkness. Then the captives heard another sound: the dry crackling of flames spreading

When famine hit the Rhineland, a cruel Bishop silenced the hungry populace. He lured them into a barn, locked the doors and set the place alight.

through kindling. Acrid smoke began to fill the barn. The first cries of panic splintered into shrieks of agony as the fire took hold. Fingers clawed blindly at the walls, but there was no way out.

From a window in his palace, the Bishop gazed down on the scene, pensive but unperturbed. He watched while the fire did its work, until the last flaming beam had pitched from the vaulted roof. Then, turning to a minion, he said, "They would eat up the grain like rats, so like rats they died." With that, he went down to dinner, and enjoyed an ample repast of seven courses, concocted by his chefs from their stocks of hoarded supplies. The next morning, Hatto rose refreshed from an untroubled sleep. He made his way to the great hall of the palace to go over the accounts of his estates, and to estimate the taxes and tithes due

to him. As he entered, something he glimpsed out of the corner of his eye stopped him in his tracks. He swung round to look at the pictures that lined the wall, a series of portraits of all the Archbishops of Mainz, of which his own likeness was the most recent and, he thought, the best. All the others were there as usual, but his was gone. Only a scrap of canvas remained to flutter in the chill breeze that stirred the morning air. Hatto gasped in anger. As he did so, a trio of rats jumped down from the picture frame and ran out through the open door.

The Bishop was still staring in astonishment at the empty frame when a servant hurried in. He brought bad tidings: The storehouses had been scavenged in the night and barely a grain of wheat was left. Hardly had the man finished speaking when a second messenger came in with even more alarming news. The rats were on the move. Driven by starvation, they had banded together by the thousands and were ravaging the countryside. And now the packs were converging from all directions and advancing on the town.

Hatto stumbled to the nearest window. It was true. The fields surrounding the town—his fields, the land his tenants worked—were black with the creatures. The advance guard of the verminous army was even now moving like a wave up the hill toward the palace, flowing over walls and hedges and erasing all signs of the road. Already they were close enough for Hatto to make out individual rats at the front of the column, twisting and bounding in the urgency of their pur-

24

While the churchman supped on hoarded grain, a pack of
rats stole into his palace and ate his portrait out of its frame.

pose and emitting a high squeaking that was horrible to hear.

For a moment Hatto stood mesmerized, but his sense of self-preservation soon spurred him to action. Ashen-faced, he turned to flee, running through the dark corridors and narrow stairways of the palace to a secret passage that led out under the ramparts. From there, he followed a path down to the Rhine. At the water's edge, the Bishop barked a command at a startled boatman, and soon the two of them were on the river, heading for an islet in midstream.

Even before the boat touched land, the Bishop had jumped out of it and was scrambling over the rocks to an old stone tower that he used in happier times as a summer retreat. Bursting into the refuge, he paused only to bar the door firmly behind him, then leaped up the spiraling stairs two by two. When at last he reached the uppermost room of the aerie, he collapsed, panting, on a cot to recover his breath and his wits.

He was not to rest for long. The horrible squealing and shuffling of the rodent horde still echoed in his ears; but then he realized it was getting louder. Forcing himself to a window, he found himself staring down on a sea of rats, swarming down the hill from the palace walls, bobbing in the current as they cleaved their way through the Rhine waters, and clustering in a pulsating mass around the foot of the building. As he watched, the first rats started nimbly to claw their way up the sheer stone walls. The rest followed, and soon a rising mantle of heaving fur enveloped the tower.

Turning away from the window, the Bishop sank to his knees. Fear would have prevented him from running, even had there been anywhere to hide. Without conscious volition he found his hands working his rosary beads, his lips muttering half-forgotten snatches of prayer.

Within seconds the rats were in the room. Slithering and squeaking, their fur still matted with river water, they surrounded the bed on which the Bishop lay. Pink muzzles twitched; hungry eyes glinted for vengeance. The air was filled with the scratching of their restless paws on the floorboards and their high, thin and incessant squeaking.

Frozen with terror, Hatto could not move a muscle, save those of his eyes. The creatures were all around him now, thrusting their quivering snouts so close that the bristles stroked his flesh. They were scenting him like carrion. Heads raised, they showed their long, yellow incisors, and the stench of death was on their breath. One leaped at Hatto's face. Some last instinct of survival triggered a response, and he clawed the beast away. But then the whole pack moved, up and over the cot, covering it and its occupant beneath a seething blanket.

When attendants found the body of the Bishop later in the day, it was picked clean to the bone. There was no sign of the rats. They had disappeared as suddenly and mysteriously as they had come. Their bellies were full at last.

From all the empty granaries came thousands of rodents on the march.
They stalked the Bishop to his hiding-place, overcame him by force
of numbers, and sated their hunger on his well-nourished flesh.

In the Body of the Beast

The Jewish storytellers of Eastern Europe told of a certain blighted era in the history of Poland—a time when foreign armies dismembered the country, bands of thugs raped and murdered their way through the poorest settlements, and cholera decimated the survivors. By cruel coincidence, the weather visited unprecedented hardship on the land—a succession of sunless summers, ruinous autumn storms and winters cold enough to kill.

It seemed, said the sages, that Satan himself had enfolded the earth in a pair of iron wings, blocking out the light from heaven. At times he came even closer, walking the world to sow sin and horror. But once, according to a story that circulated among the poor, he was challenged by a youth who possessed rare powers and the aura of perfect innocence. His name was Israel, and he was an orphan, dependent for survival on his own wits and the charity of others. When still barely more than a child himself, he earned his keep by escorting the young pupils of his village to and from the school next to the synagogue.

In those days, among the Jews, children were rarely allowed to wander freely. Parents feared for the safety of their offspring. When they left the warmth of their mothers' kitchens, they did so bedecked with amulets and sprinkled with blessings to ward off disease, disaster and the evil eye.

It soon became known that young Israel did not simply take his charges to school and back again. He made unscheduled detours. After classes had finished, he led his little band of scholars on daily rambles through the woods, to point out a bird's nest full of eggs, to admire a butterfly, to gather mushrooms and taste the fruits of the forest. He showed the children that trees, plants and wild flowers were, in their own ways, as holy as the written scriptures. While roaming among the trees, Israel entertained them with riddles and stories, and taught them the only songs that he knew, which were hymns of praise. The tunes were simple, the lyrics easy to remember.

But the children's parents were appalled to learn of Israel's forays into the forest. They were people who passed the greater part of their lives in stuffy rooms, behind the closed doors of home or synagogue or study-house. One by one, as Israel brought each child home at twilight, the angry mothers confronted him, demanding explanations. Yet such was his air of preternatural wisdom that he was able to reassure them that their young ones would be perfectly safe in his hands. They wanted to believe this, because they saw the new bloom in their children's cheeks and hoped that some good might come of it.

The parents would have been less acquiescent if they had realized that the deep woods housed something dangerous. In the heart of the forest lived an old woodcutter with a strange affliction: Every night, demons entered his body and made free with it. At their compulsion, he crouched on all fours, howled like a wolf and pursued the small woodland creatures to tear their throats out.

By day and by nature the woodcutter was a simple man, who bore no malice to anyone. Mortified by the fits that came upon him, he hid himself away from humankind. The sound of Israel and the children singing in the forest might have soothed his sorrow, but the devils who enslaved him were not pleased to be assailed by hymns in piping voices. These lesser demons carried word of the intrusion to Satan himself. Sensing a threat, the King of Evil decided that he, and not his minions, should grapple with the adolescent holy man.

One midnight, when the woodcutter moaned and mumbled in his nightmares, Satan entered the werewolf's

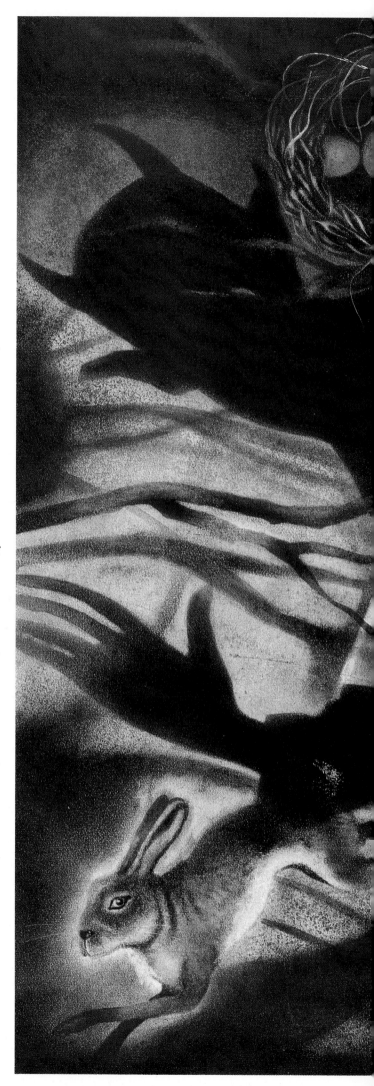

body, removed his troubled heart, and replaced it with his own. This time, when the first rays of morning came, the monster remained a monster.

When Israel and his young companions entered the woods, intent on a second breakfast of wild berries, something had changed in the forest. No birds sang, no breeze stirred the leaves or rustled in the pine needles. Israel sniffed the air and listened, until the sound of the children's laughter shattered the silence. They had found a clump of bushes heavy with ripe fruit and now they were busy filling their mouths and pockets.

Suddenly the innermost branches began to rustle and shiver. The werewolf burst out of the thicket, roaring and slavering. The children scattered, yet the boy Israel stood his ground. The beast came closer, swelling up until it blotted out all sight of the leaden sky. On its breath the monster carried the reek of the blood that had been shed in all the wars since time began, the stale stench of hunger, the rankness of sin. In its eyes were reflected scenes of carnage, horsemen swooping low to tear infants from their mothers' arms, babies impaled on the points of bayonets. Israel recited every prayer he knew. But the words glanced off the beast's hide like harmless sparks. Then Israel began to hum one of the old tunes he had taught the children. The werewolf opened its jaw as wide as the gates of hell and prepared to swallow him.

For what happened next, the chroniclers had only Israel's word, but they faithfully recounted it. The youth walked into the maw of the beast. Shielded by his piety, Israel became aware of forces far beyond his ken. He found himself in a place where the laws of nature had no meaning: Some power, divine or diabolic, had altered all perspective and proportion. He moved through the body of the beast as if through a dark corridor, drawn by the sound of a distant drumbeat. The pounding grew steadily louder and more insistent. It summoned him to a great cavern, awash with blood and walled by bone. There, suspended from the branches of a tree of flesh, was the creature's heart—not the heart of the woodcutter, nor the heart of a wolf, but the heart of all the evil alive in the world: alluring as a mirror, cold and adamantine to the touch.

A person of less courage might have recoiled in horror from the thing as they would from a coiled-up adder; a person of less wisdom might have rashly tried to wrench its lobes apart. But Israel raised an arm, drew down the dangling heart and held it close to his ear. Within its depths, nearly drowned out by the insistent hammering of hate, he heard something soft and secret: a whisper of sorrow, a whimper of distress. Then Israel understood that even in the core of evil itself, there was also suffering and pain. No malign spirit, fiend or demon was invulnerable.

Gently, as if removing the dead head of a rose, he plucked the object free, cradled it in his palms and walked out again into the light. But when he emerged from the body of the beast, the ground trembled beneath his feet and thunder cleaved the sky. A fissure yawned suddenly in the forest floor. The heart slipped from his hand and rolled into the chasm. Then the earth closed over it.

Israel stood before the corpse. What previously had been a werewolf, fanged, furred and beclawed, was now only the body of the gentle old woodcutter, his ravaged face transformed by death. He lay still and smiling, suffused with a saint's tranquility.

Israel drew forth his blue and white striped prayer shawl from his pocket, draped it around his shoulders and began to intone the sacred words of the kaddish—the ancient Hebrew chant of mourning. When he had finished, he looked up to see the village children standing behind him, silent and with stricken faces. He tried to tell them what he had learned inside the belly of the beast, thinking these discoveries might bring them courage and comfort, but they did not stay to listen. From that day forward they never walked in the woods again, seldom sang, and became, like their parents, old before their time.

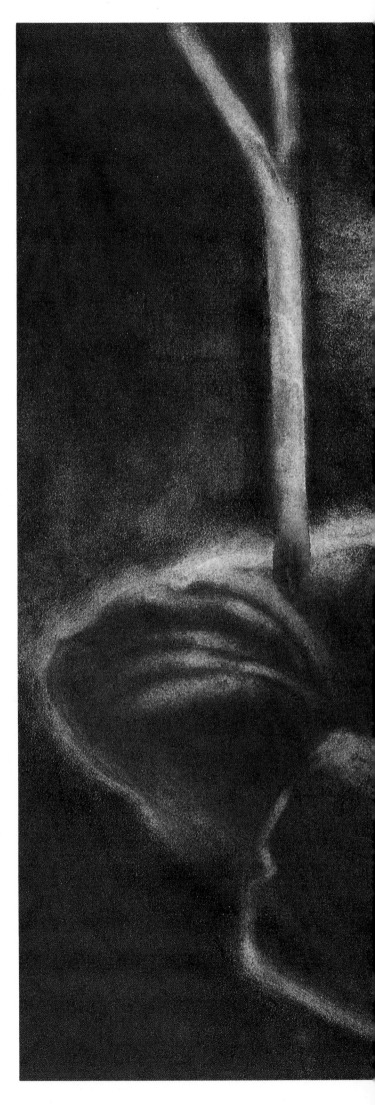

Thorgunna, a Hebridean woman, came to lodge on a bleak Icelandic farm,
bringing with her a chest of handsome bed linen. Her hostess, Thurid,
ached to possess the goods, but Thorgunna would not sell at any price.

·4·

Harvest of Horrors

In the waning days of the old gods, the inhabitants of an isolated Icelandic farm fell prey to a terrifying series of hauntings. The events began innocently enough with the appearance of a traveler named Thorgunna. She had come from the Hebrides, isles of stones and secrets far to the south. Like many people of her time, she was a wanderer on the seas, moving restlessly from place to place, making her home wherever she found herself. She carried with her two trunks containing her worldly goods.

The old Norse storytellers did not explain how she came to lodge at the farm called Froda, on a peninsula jutting out into the black Atlantic. It may have been a distant kinsman of the farmer, dwelling on the shores of Vatersay or in the peaty wastes of Lewis, who sent her there with gifts and messages of greeting. She was kindly received by Froda's master and given a cool welcome by Thurid, his wife. Yet her hostess warmed considerably when the visitor unpacked her belongings. All the women of the large household gathered around to watch, lured by the prospect of something new and pretty.

They were a disparate lot, drawn together by the fates: Some were cousins, others slaves, still others the wives of men pledged to fight alongside the master of Froda in times of war. Thurid looked on, and ached with longing for the sheets of English linen, the hangings of rich brocades, the coverlet of Eastern silk, even the down-stuffed mattress and pillows, for nothing like them had ever been seen in the neighborhood before. Thurid had never been one to bandy words: She asked Thorgunna to name her price. The newcomer laughed,

Falling on the fields during haymaking, a rainstorm of blood
soaked the grass and stained the garments of Thorgunna, marking
her out as a victim of the gods' displeasure. She was doomed.

and inquired why she should sleep on a bed of straw and let Thurid lie in luxury. The onlookers hid their smiles behind their hands, amused to see their proud mistress for once put in her place.

Although she had gold enough to pay for her lodging, Thorgunna preferred to work for her keep by helping about the farm—weaving when the weather was wet, raking hay when it was dry. With her tart tongue and reserved manner, she made few friends. Worse, she was a follower of the alien faith that threatened Odin and Thor's ancient hegemony.

Each morning she went alone to pray in an abandoned stone chapel built by Irish monks, who had dwelled in the land before the Viking settlers came. The womenfolk of Froda muttered that no good could come of this. Then, during the haymaking, the old gods unleashed their anger.

On a brilliantly clear day, as the men and women of Froda turned and raked the hay to dry it more quickly, a storm blew up out of nowhere. Oblivious to the deluge, Thorgunna continued turning and spreading the hay as the rains poured down. But those around her dropped their implements in horror: The precipitation was blood. Scarlet rivulets raced down Thorgunna's arms, pooled at her feet, and stained the hay as she spread it. When she saw herself coated in gore, Thorgunna shrieked. The people backed away, murmuring among themselves, and the cloud vanished as quickly as it had come. The field soon dried, except for

the patch where Thorgunna had been at work. There the hay lay dark and glistening, and Thorgunna, her clothes dripping blood and sweat, leaned exhausted against her rake. All her strength and vitality had been sapped by the passing cloud. Even her glossy chestnut hair hung lank beneath her scarf.

When Thorgunna cried out that the rain foretold death, people nodded in agreement. The Old Ones sometimes sent such portents as signs that a mortal's time on earth was soon to end.

That night, Thorgunna removed her reddened, reeking garments and, with a sigh that had the weariness of death in it, took to her bed. The others in the large household whispered among themselves, watched and waited, their eyes shining in the firelight. The next morning, for the first time since her arrival, Thorgunna did not go to the stone chapel to say her strange Christian prayers.

Only the master of Froda came to her bedside to ask about her illness. The others had felt the lash of her harsh tongue too often to risk prying. Thorgunna announced that she was dying and asked him, as head of the household, to carry out her last wishes.

The sick woman told him that she wanted him to convey her body to Skalholt, where the community of Christian monks could offer up prayers for her soul. Then she decreed the disposal of her belongings after her death. The Skalholt monks were to have her gold ring, and the farmer was to recompense himself for the cost of the journey by taking in payment a fine silver brooch. Thurid was to have a red cape to stop her from interfering. All the rest of her possessions were

When Thorgunna sickened and died, Thurid ignored her last instructions for the disposal of her worldly goods. She seized the fine bedclothes before their owner's corpse was cold.

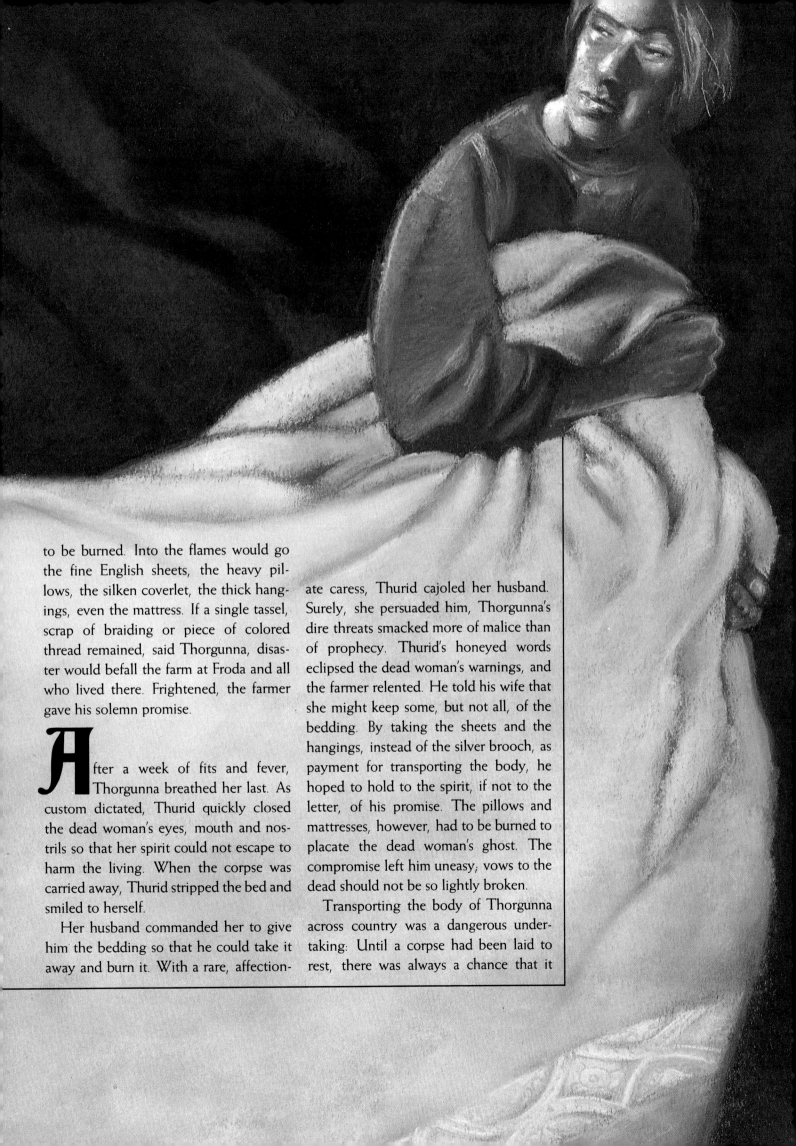

to be burned. Into the flames would go the fine English sheets, the heavy pillows, the silken coverlet, the thick hangings, even the mattress. If a single tassel, scrap of braiding or piece of colored thread remained, said Thorgunna, disaster would befall the farm at Froda and all who lived there. Frightened, the farmer gave his solemn promise.

After a week of fits and fever, Thorgunna breathed her last. As custom dictated, Thurid quickly closed the dead woman's eyes, mouth and nostrils so that her spirit could not escape to harm the living. When the corpse was carried away, Thurid stripped the bed and smiled to herself.

Her husband commanded her to give him the bedding so that he could take it away and burn it. With a rare, affectionate caress, Thurid cajoled her husband. Surely, she persuaded him, Thorgunna's dire threats smacked more of malice than of prophecy. Thurid's honeyed words eclipsed the dead woman's warnings, and the farmer relented. He told his wife that she might keep some, but not all, of the bedding. By taking the sheets and the hangings, instead of the silver brooch, as payment for transporting the body, he hoped to hold to the spirit, if not to the letter, of his promise. The pillows and mattresses, however, had to be burned to placate the dead woman's ghost. The compromise left him uneasy; vows to the dead should not be so lightly broken.

Transporting the body of Thorgunna across country was a dangerous undertaking. Until a corpse had been laid to rest, there was always a chance that it

might rise up in its shroud to walk again. With the heavy bundle strapped to the back of an ox, a small band of men and women set off across the moors to the monastery. The fine summer weather had ended abruptly with the shower of blood; a cold, wet wind blew in from the Arctic, signaling the start of the long winter. As the funeral party trudged on, the body began to show signs of having a will of its own. It slipped from side to side on the ox, no matter how tightly the ropes were tied to secure it. It grew heavier with each step; the ox slowed and finally came to a halt, impervious to the touch of its master's whip.

Night was falling, but the lights of a farmhouse were in sight. As carriers of a corpse to burial, the group was owed proper hospitality—hot food, dry clothes and the warmest place by the fire. But the master of that place was a miser and offered them only the poorest shelter, refusing them all else. Unable to go any farther, the party settled down for the night far from the fire, bellies rumbling beneath their sodden clothes.

Before anyone could sleep, noises were heard coming from the kitchen. When the head of the household went in to confront the intruder, he found the shrouded corpse of Thorgunna moving about, preparing supper for her pallbearers. Grave clothes flapping, she took provisions from the amply stocked cupboard and set a fine meal on the table. Anxious to satisfy the ghost's wishes and thus avert any curse on his crops and livestock, the farmer invited the travelers to eat and make themselves comfortable.

The party approached the table and looked suspiciously at the provisions the dead woman had prepared. Fearing the power of the revenant, the farmer muttered an incantation over the dishes. Then he begged the men and women of Froda to sit down to their meal. Their master was the first to raise a morsel to his lips. The others watched as he ate. Seeing that the ghost's offering caused no ill effects, the others at first warily, then hungrily, attacked the food. Thorgunna, appeased, returned to her coffin.

Word of what had happened spread quickly throughout the district, and for the duration of the journey the corpse-bearers were met with the finest hospitality the rugged land had to offer. Everyone was afraid of the dead woman, but so long as her wishes were respected, she was content to lie quiet.

At the monastery, the monks took Thorgunna's golden ring and her soul into their care and consigned her earthly remains to the graveyard to await Judgment Day. Freed of their obligations, the people of Froda retraced their steps to the farm. On the party's first night home, the household sat around the long fire in the main room. Gossip picked up on the journey to the monastery was passed on to the people who had stayed behind, for any news of the world outside the closed circle of the farm was welcome. Within the confines of the thick sod walls, the thirty men, women and children who lived there raked over old scandals and plotted new revenges, fought

Bearing the dead woman to a distant burial ground, the funeral party stopped to rest at a farm. There, the ghost of Thorgunna emerged from the shadows to serve them supper.

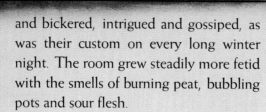

and bickered, intrigued and gossiped, as was their custom on every long winter night. The room grew steadily more fetid with the smells of burning peat, bubbling pots and sour flesh.

The desultory conversation around the fireside was brought to a sudden halt. A beam of light, from an unknown source, floated across the walls from corner to corner. All eyes followed the glowing semicircle as it spun slowly from right to left around the room. An old crone cried out that it was the Moon of Urd, goddess of fate—a harbinger of doom. Worse still, it was traveling widdershins—in the opposite direction to the sun—a sure sign that it came from the dark powers that ruled the night. Another woman, equally versed in the black arts, shuddered and said that she felt death in the house, stalking all its occupants. Thorgunna did not lie easy in her grave.

For an entire week, the moon appeared each night and spun dizzily backward around the room. On the eighth night, as the household sat in the long room, staring at the walls and waiting for the weird shadow to appear, the outer door flew open and the shepherd who tended the Froda flock rushed in out of the night. His eyes were wild with fear and his movements convulsive. He avoided people's gaze and swore at anyone who came near him. Everyone left him alone, for the big man had a violent temper. Then he babbled out an incoherent story of the dangers outside in the dark, and ran screaming back to the sheepfold.

Every night for a fortnight the shepherd came bursting into the house with yet another account of something, never specified, that threatened him out on the moors. One morning, a group of men found him stiff and dead in his hut, but without a mark on his body. They buried him that same day, in the empty chapel, with stones piled high on his chest to keep him in his grave.

That night, someone banged on the walls of the house and threw clods of dirt against the door. One of the women opened it, then banged it shut: The corpse of the shepherd was on the rampage. For many nights thereafter, he rode the roof of the house, thumping his heels against the beams and howling at the moon. His nails clawed the walls and scratched at the door as he searched for others to join him beyond the grave. No one ventured outside after sunset, for the darkness belonged to him. Spells were muttered against the shepherd and talismans clutched in trembling hands.

One night, shortly after dusk, a series of sickening thuds resounded against the house. The specter, immune to spells and amulets, had attacked one of the men returning from the fields and flung him, over and over again, at the outer walls. Gasping out a charm to banish the walking dead, the injured man crawled toward the door, his ribs crushed and his head dripping blood. Although his wife was known to be a skillful witch, none of her magic could cure him.

When at last he died, his body was placed next to the shepherd's grave in the long-abandoned church. From that time

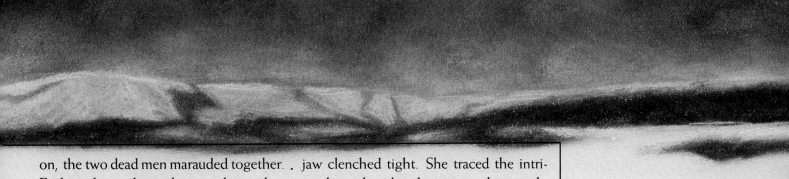

on, the two dead men marauded together. .
Each night in the gathering gloom they
lurked, still and menacing, at the edge of
the meadow, waiting for more of the living to join them.

Within the farmhouse, there were
other disturbances. Inexplicable rustling,
scratching and ripping noises were heard
issuing from the cupboard where they
kept the stock of dried fish for the winter.
Whenever anyone looked inside, nothing
could be seen but the stacked slabs of
dried and salted cod.

The house was under siege by the
walking dead. Its occupants were hollow-
eyed from lack of sleep, and quick to
anger. A quarrel claimed one life, chills
and agues another. Soon a growing crowd
of revenants clustered outside the walls,
muttering threats and imprecations.

Except for a few hours in the middle of
the day, the darkness and its creatures
ruled over Froda farm. The oxen in their
pens bellowed and kicked their heels
against the wooden fences as the dead
men mounted and rode them. Unseen
hands drew the milk from the cows over-
night. Each morning the beasts were
thinner, their eyes rolling with fear in
the watery winter light.

Thurid became very quiet. As though
sharing a guilty secret, she and her husband avoided looking one another in the
eye. They circled warily around one another, careful not to touch in the close
confines of the long, narrow room. All
through the endless hours of waiting and
listening, Thurid sat on her stool and
stroked Thorgunna's splendid bedclothes,
while her husband stood watching, his

jaw clenched tight. She traced the intricately embroidered patterns, her work-
worn hands caressing the cloth as she
counted the minute stitches.

The sounds coming from within the
fish cupboard grew louder by the day.
Everyone began to worry about their
winter food supply. Even if the fish were
not being eaten, they were sure to be
contaminated by the presence of the unseen intruder. The master of the farm decided to travel to a nearby fishing-port to
buy more cod. Gathering together five of
the strongest men, he set off in a fleet,
ten-oared craft. The trip would be a risky
one, so near the winter solstice, for the
sea was rough, the skies dark and the evil
spirits out in force.

In the farmhouse that evening, after
the fire had been lighted and people were
beginning to gather, a servant girl let out
a sudden shriek and dropped a basin of
gruel. She pointed to something rising
out of the floor. It was the gray head of
a seal. And, despite its ability to rise
through solid, hard-packed earth and rush
matting, it was no apparition.

Seizing a club, the girl began to
batter the intruder. But the creature's slippery body continued to push up
through the floor. The seal turned baleful eyes to Thurid's bed, staring with
an almost human expression at Thorgunna's stolen hangings, sheets and coverlet.
With each stroke of the club, the creature rose higher and higher until its flip-
pers dripped dark puddles on the floor.
The servant fell back in a faint; the rest

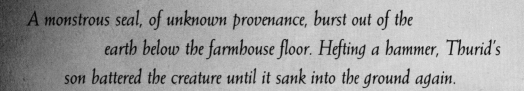

*A monstrous seal, of unknown provenance, burst out of the
earth below the farmhouse floor. Hefting a hammer, Thurid's
son battered the creature until it sank into the ground again.*

of the household stood paralyzed. Nothing seemed able to stop the unholy beast.

Kjartan, Thurid's son, shouldered his way through the crowd, holding a stone-headed hammer. He raised it high, then slammed it down on the creature's skull. The seal shook its gray head, shivered its whiskers and gazed around the room. Kjartan continued his savage hammering, aiming blow after blow at the head. His breathing grew heavy and uneven, his body glistened with sweat as he put all his youthful strength behind the hammer.

Finally, the seal slipped back down into the darkness and disappeared. Still Kjartan did not stop, but kept on until the floor itself was pounded flat and smooth again. The people backed away from the violated spot, muttering that even the house was no longer safe from the incursions of the evil ones.

Worse was to come. The next day, a fisherman brought news that Froda's master and his companions had perished in the stormy seas. Their boat was found upside down but undamaged, and the boxes containing the newly purchased fish had floated to shore on the tides.

Kjartan and Thurid were determined that their dead should be honored properly. Despite the fear and chaos in the house, they invited the neighbors to a funeral banquet. They brought out the ale that had been set aside for the winter solstice and prepared enough food to entertain the guests for a week.

On the first night of the feast, as the guests sat around the long fire, ale cups in

All the dead of Froda farm, victims of violence and disease alike,
came forth in winter nights to share the food and fire of the living.

their hands, the outer door swung open and a chill, wet wind blew into the hall. The drowned men filed in. They had come back to attend their own funeral. Their skin was wrinkled and bloated from immersion in the frigid brine. Water dripped from their clothes and hair, and their boots squelched on the floor. With miserable expressions, they rubbed cold, pale hands and headed toward the fire.

They stayed near the hearth, warming their hands, the steam rising from their wet garments. The living members of the household cowered in the shadows: They knew that shipwrecked sailors favored by Ran, goddess of the sea, were sometimes allowed a last visit to their homes before their hair turned to seaweed and their skin to jelly. Then, as soundlessly as they had arrived, the dead departed, still oozing slime and sea water.

The next night, they reappeared as soon as the fire was lighted. For the rest of the week, while the funeral feast continued, so too did the hauntings. Some of the guests maintained that once the funeral was over, the dead would stay beneath the waves. But on the first night after the guests had gone home, the drowned men came back again.

This time they were not alone. As soon as the dripping corpses had seated themselves by the blazing fire, the dead from the cemetery joined them, shedding bits of the frozen earth that clung to their shrouds. As long as the fire burned, the dead occupied the room while the living shivered in an unheated antechamber.

After that night, Kjartan ordered that a fire be made in the other room as well. Each night, when the dead took over the main room, the living huddled together around the smaller fire. And so the old year and the weeks beyond it passed.

During the months of the hauntings, the ripping and tearing noises from the fish cupboard grew louder. One night, when a servant went to take some of the fish from the store, she saw a long, thin tail covered with short, smooth hair lying atop the slabs of salt cod. The tail was blackened and scorched, and tipped with fringes. She grabbed hold of it and called to the others, guessing that the tail belonged to the creature that had been making all the noise amid the dried fish.

Everyone came running and grabbed the tail. Although they used all their strength, they could not pull its owner out of the fish heap. With a movement as swift as lightning, the tail flew out of their hands, burning their palms and ripping off the tender skin, wrenching cries of pain from their throats. Hundreds of fish skins fell onto the floor with an empty, rustling sound. The invisible creature had sucked out flesh, leaving only skin and bones behind.

With the fish stores destroyed and the dead in control each night, a new attack of illnesses swept the farm. The witch woman was the first to be stricken, and the dead quickly took her for their own. Buried deep under the earth one morning, she was seen walking the dark paths around the farm that night, arm in arm with her husband—who had been killed months before by the berserk

Beneath the winter stockpiles of
dried cod, something unseen thrashed its long
and sinuous tail. When it departed,
the members of the household found that the
mysterious predator had eaten the flesh
clean off the fishbones.

shepherd. Finally only seven people were left. Thurid became ill and hid beneath Thorgunna's silken coverlet, the brocade curtains pulled tight around her bed.

In the first lengthening days after midwinter, Kjartan went to ask his mother's brother for advice. Snorri was the head of his clan, a man as much respected for his sense of justice and his knowledge of the law as for his cunning and his ability to get the better of an enemy.

Snorri listened carefully to Kjartan's account of the winter hauntings. He considered what was to be done. He told Kjartan that all the trouble stemmed from the breaking of the promises his father had made to the Hebridean woman on her deathbed. If the last wishes of a dying person were not obeyed, the ghost would never rest. All the things that she had asked to be burned must be destroyed. Once that happened, Thorgunna would lie quiet in her grave. The other revenants who walked the farm could only be exorcised by being tried in a court of law. They had to be charged with their crimes of murder and trespass, found guilty and dispatched to the afterworld. Snorri told Kjartan that he should take a Christian priest back with him to the farm. Once the priest had overseen the exorcisms, he could sprinkle his holy water about the house in order to cleanse it of its evil spirits. Kjartan, the

priest and some others set off that day. On his return, Kjartan found that his mother was still clinging to life. By this time, Thurid was so weak that not a word of protest escaped her lips when Kjartan ripped the sheets and blankets from the bed on which she lay. Wrenching the hangings from the wall, he took a flaming brand from the fireplace and went outside to burn the cursed goods.

First the fragile silks burned, turning the flames all the brilliant colors of the Orient. The thick woolens smoldered and smoked before catching fire. Finally the coverlets were added, and the air was filled with the acrid smell of burning feathers. In the glare of the flames, Kjartan thought he saw a flash of chestnut hair. Next, he prepared to try the dead for their crimes, under the brilliant moon. He summoned the corpses from the churchyard and from the sea to the farmhouse. As they drew near, Kjartan steeled himself for the task ahead.

With a steady voice and a pounding heart, Kjartan called the dead men and women to the seat of judgment. The charges against them were read out— murder, trespass, unlawful killing—and the verdict of guilty was passed. The dead were sentenced one by one to banishment. With downcast faces, they each came forward and accepted their sentence. They may have been cowed by the presence of an alien priest, for none complained, but shuffled off without a word to their final resting-places. The hauntings at the farm of Froda were over.

·5·

The Goblins' Guest

In the lost ages before Emperors ruled Japan, the land was trouble-torn and haunted. By day, rival warlords fought for power. The swords of their samurai whistled on the battleground, and the blood from heaped corpses stained the paddy fields. But at night there were quieter armies on the march—battalions of shape-shifting demons, spectral foxes, vengeful ghosts oozing up from hell.

Each evening, those with homes to go to hid behind barred doors until dawn. But some mortals were compelled by bad luck or poverty to pass the nights exposed to the dangers of the dark. Those who survived had harrowing tales to tell.

One account concerned a priest named Kwairyo. In his youth he had been a samurai, sworn to the service of a feudal lord. There was none more skilled or scrupulous than he in the arts and rituals of combat. But the shifting tides of war brought ruin to his noble master. Rather than serve another earthly chief, Kwairyo became a soldier of heaven and took to the roads to spread the holy word.

Once, while traveling through a wild and mountainous region, he was stranded halfway between two remote hamlets as darkness fell. A storm wind battered the hills, but he was far from any safe shelter.

Kwairyo wrapped himself in his cloak and sought a resting-place under the dripping pines. As he searched, he encountered a woodcutter bearing an ax and a bundle of branches. Greeting Kwairyo courteously, the rustic asked what a holy man was doing out alone on such a wild night. Was he not afraid of the demons that could suck a man's soul out through his ears? Did he wish to become a mindless husk, wandering maze-eyed through the fields, shouting folly to the winds?

The woodcutter invited Kwairyo to take refuge at his house in the forest. It was but a miserable hovel, he added, but it provided a roof against the rain, and a fire in the hearth to keep evil at bay. Kwairyo accepted with thanks. He followed the woodcutter along forest tracks, skirting steep precipices and gorges.

The cottage lay at the bottom of a slope, its windows bright and welcoming. A waterfall descended from the hillside, flowing like an old man's beard to feed a bamboo aqueduct behind the house, and

Stranded in the wilderness during a storm, a Japanese holy man encountered a woodcutter. Courteously, the rustic offered him shelter against the perils of the night.

a cedar grove stood nearby. Bowing, the woodsman opened the door for his guest. Inside, two men and two women crouched around a fireplace in the center of the room, where a simmering kettle sent forth the pungent odor of dragon-eye tea. The four rose and greeted Kwairyo with words and gestures more suited to a palace than to a hut in the woods.

After taking tea, Kwairyo questioned his host about his origins. The woodcutter answered that once he had been a military commander, victor in many battles fought for a mighty lord. But he had strayed from the strict moral code of the samurai, accepted bribes and gambled heavily. Debauchery had made him careless, and one night an enemy attack caught him unaware. His soldiers perished and his lord was overthrown. In penance he had exiled himself to this remote district. He and his companions spent their days aiding the lost and needy.

Full of fellow feeling for a brother samurai brought low, the priest promised to spend the night in prayer on his host's behalf. The woodcutter led Kwairyo to an alcove concealed behind a screen, and left him to his devotions.

As the hours passed, the fire sank to embers, casting the faint shadows of five whispering figures against the paper wall. But still Kwairyo sat upright, intoning the sacred words. Finally, he felt sleep overtaking him. He rose and opened the window. The storm was over. The priest's throat was dry from chanting and the very sight and sound of the waterfall made him thirsty. He decided to slip out to get a drink from the aqueduct outside. He crept to the door of the house and silently opened it. There, on the ground in front of him, he saw five recumbent bodies. Just then the moon emerged from the clouds, illuminating the sleepers. He stared for a moment in disbelief.

The bodies at Kwairyo's feet were headless. He wondered if bandits had attacked, but the necks showed no blood, nor any signs of violence. Not even the sharpest blade, wielded by the most skillful swordsman, could leave such smooth and unpuckered cuts.

If he had not been bred to look fear in the face, Kwairyo would have turned and fled. For these mutilated forms could be nothing other than *rokuro-kubi*, goblins of the dark. By day they resembled ordinary humans. Outwardly they gave no sign that they were bloodless, that only bile and venom coursed through their veins. But at night, so it was said, their heads floated free of their bodies.

Drifting through the darkness, guided by the demoniac light glowing from their eye sockets, the goblin heads went hunting. They wandered the countryside, hungry for living flesh. It was said that the only way to destroy such a goblin was to hide its body while the head was on its travels. Unable to return home, the head would scream out its fury until the dawn's first rays made it shrivel and die.

Thinking to use this ploy, Kwairyo seized the body of the woodcutter and dragged it away. He buried it in a ditch, under a pile of leaves and soft loam. He heard a sound in the nearby cedar grove:

Unable to believe his own eyes' evidence, the priest kneeled to
scrutinize the bodies of his hosts. All five heads were missing.

a hissing, barely discernible above the song of the cicadas and the gentle bubbling of the bamboo aqueduct. He moved toward the noise, slipping from tree to tree. Then he saw his quarry, illuminated by fitful moonlight as clouds blew across the sky.

Five heads bobbed on the ground in the clearing, grazing on the night insects and small creeping things. They gobbled and snorted as they fed, taking in mouthfuls of earth along with the grubs. Their teeth were obscured by strands of leaf mold and the hard, indigestible husks of beetles that had fallen prey to their greedy maws. The head of the woodcutter, larger than the others, hissed furiously as it flitted to and fro.

The monk could hear the heads quarreling loudly among themselves as they crunched the bones of still-squirming voles and squirrels. They cursed the woodcutter for bringing the holy man into the house. How stupid he had been to bid for sympathy with that story of his downfall. If only the man were not at that moment praying for their souls, he would be an easy target, far more delectable than their present fare.

One of the female heads rose from the ground and flew, light as a bat, to the house, to see if their guest had fallen asleep at his devotions. While it was gone, the other heads continued foraging. Sticky loops of saliva dribbled from their jaws as they argued over who should

In a moonlit clearing, a pack of disembodied heads
gobbled insects. Through mouths full
of half-chewed carapaces, they gibbered curses
and clamored for human flesh.

have first choice of the priest's tenderest portions. But a moment later, the head returned in panic. The priest, it said, was nowhere to be found and, worse still, the woodcutter's body had vanished.

The others hovered in confusion about the head of the woodcutter. It began to quiver and gyrate, its cheeks ballooning, its tongue snaking out from between empurpled lips. Its eyes glowed scarlet. The hair rose and rippled, as if transformed into a mass of elvers writhing in a net.

"If I die," the disembodied woodcutter shrieked, "then the priest dies with me."

Kwairyo darted deeper into the trees, but his white robe had flashed for an instant in the moonlight, and the great red eyes swiveled in his direction. Like a pack of hounds on the track of a wounded deer, the heads flew at Kwairyo.

Casting about for a weapon, he saw a small sapling and plucked it, roots and all, from the earth. As the heads came at him, he swung the young tree round like a cudgel, dealing each a blow that sent it spinning into the darkness. Four of the heads fled, unable to take the battering, but still the face of the woodcutter danced before him, darting and snapping. Back and forth they battled, Kwairyo making swipes with his sapling as the head weaved and bobbed.

Suddenly, the head slipped under his guard and made straight for his throat. Remembering an old trick of the samurai, Kwairyo dropped to one side and raised his arm in defense. The teeth missed their target but fastened instead onto the sleeve of his robe. And there the bodiless creature hung, worrying away at the cloth.

Kwairyo's arm rose and fell as he tried to shake off the head, banging it against tree trunks and rocks. At last, the head ceased to struggle and stared, glassy-eyed, at the moon. Rivulets of slime oozed from all its orifices. Try as he might, he was unable to dislodge the creature's teeth from the rough hessian of his robe. Twice he sought to remove the garment, but each time he began to draw his arm out of the sleeve, the head swiveled round and bit him in the wrist.

He ran to the house, where he found the other four goblins reunited with their bodies. They clustered together, licking and nuzzling at each other's wounds. As Kwairyo entered, they screamed a barrage of obscenities, then plunged out of the window and disappeared.

Kwairyo struggled to retrace his route to the last village he had visited. But whichever way he turned, he came up against unbridgeable chasms, and forest trails that led him round in circles. Behind him, he could hear faint hissing noises that might have been only the wind rustling in the pines. And at every step, the head knocked against his body, its carious grin lurching from side to side.

Finally, the eyes lost their menacing glitter and shut, in the parody of a peaceful death. Kwairyo wrenched off the robe and flung it over a precipice. For another day and night he wandered naked in the forest. Then a band of young samurai found and rescued him. Having heard his story, they laughed and said privation had driven the old priest mad.

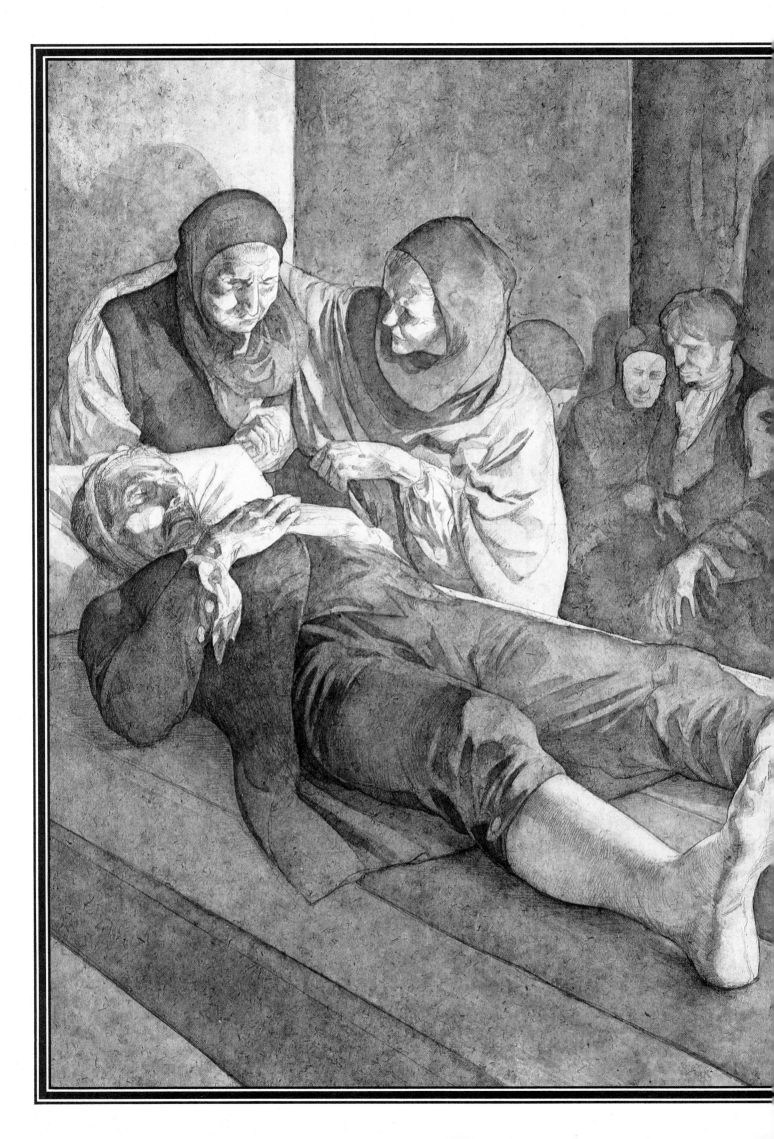

·6·

An Unfinished Death

When the coffin lid banged shut upon a corpse, it marked the slamming of the door between the worlds of dead and living. That portal opened only in one direction, and none might learn what lay beyond until their own last day and hour. But there were always those of inquiring mind who, undeterred by ancient taboo, craved to uncover these secrets. In northern Italy the tale was told of an old peasant couple, dwelling in a remote hill village, who made a pact to help each other penetrate the mystery. Sitting one night by the fire, talking of life and death, they swore a solemn vow: Whoever went first to the land of mists should return to tell the other what waited beyond the grave.

On a gray morning some years later, the husband, gathering chestnuts, fell to the earth with a gentle moan as his heart failed. Neighbors helped the weeping widow to wash the body, bind the lower jaw, and put on his Sunday jacket and breeches with the carefully folded, unworn linen shirt that had been kept in the bottom of the chest against this day. When all that was proper had been done, friends and relatives gathered to pay their last respects and offer comfort to the bereaved wife.

The widow beseeched her fellow mourners to forgo the traditional wake;

she would pass this last night alone with her husband. She sat in a stiff upright chair and studied the face that she knew better than her own. Death had sharpened the nose and chin; the mouth was sterner than ever she had known it in life. Where, she wondered, was his spirit wandering? How, and when, would he return?

A rap at the door made her jump with such sudden alarm that her chair overturned. A tall stranger stood in the doorway. He gazed at her with pale but piercing eyes, and requested shelter for the night. The woman silently indicated the body stretched out on the table of the shadowy kitchen. Yet the stranger nodded, raised one hand and stepped inside. He righted the upturned chair and offered it to the woman; then he, too, sat down, on the other side of the corpse. He bent slightly forward, hands on knees, and stared intently into the dead man's face. In his hands he held a cane of stripped hazelwood.

Then, as if from very far away, a terrible high-pitched screaming broke the silence. As it grew louder and more shrill, the corpse began to sit up. Its face was contorted in awful agony, the lips drawn tight over yellowish teeth.

Swiftly the stranger touched the dead man's forehead with his cane. The

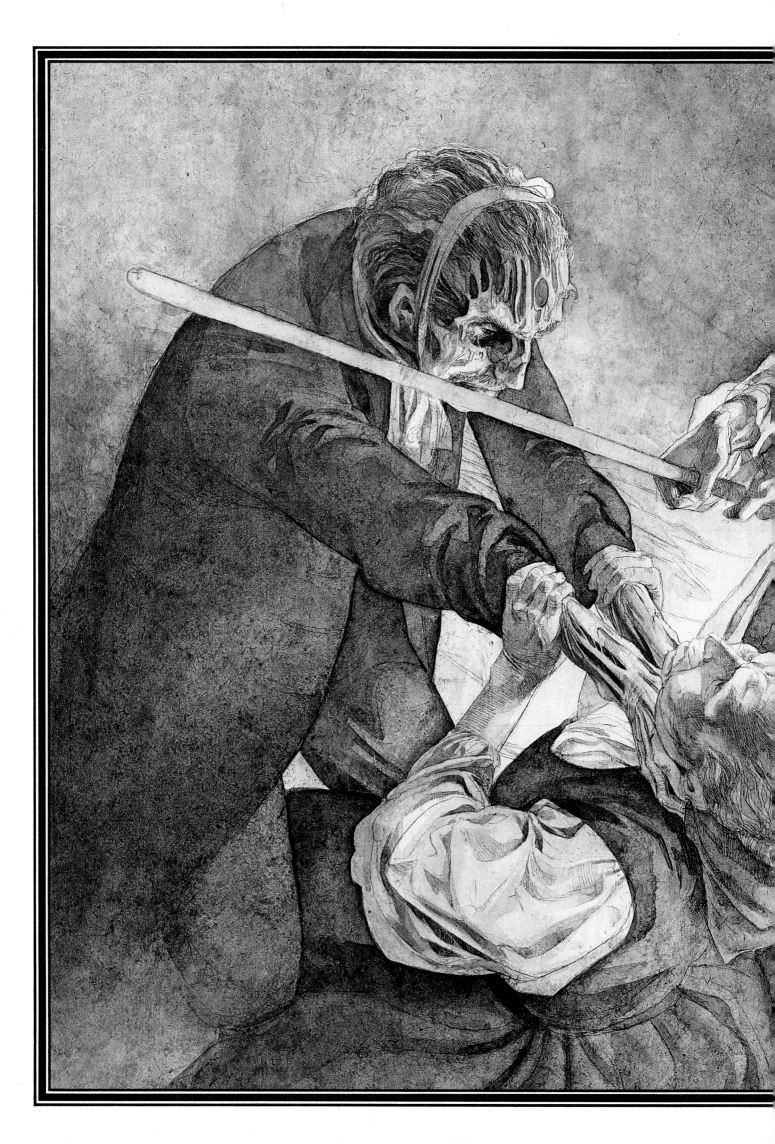

gaping mouth closed and the body prostrated itself. Stillness was restored.

The stranger resumed his seat. Minutes ticked by. The woman, her hands covering her ears, had hidden herself in an alcove. There she remained, cowering, unable to take her eyes from the cadaver's face. Then, just as her limbs had ceased to tremble, the howling began again, growing and swelling into a tidal wave of agony that engulfed every corner of the house. But, for the second time, the body prostrated itself at a touch from the stranger's cane.

The woman cringed in expectation of yet another wail, and even the distant, familiar chime of the church clock made her start. As the sound of the bell died on the air, the corpse leaped from the table. The head jerked from side to side. The bloodshot eyes bulged in their sockets. They so hypnotized the quailing widow that, like a rabbit cornered by hunters, she could not move. The body came toward her and sank hard, merciless fingers into her neck. At the same time a cracked, hollow voice cried out: "I am in hell! You put me there! I'll make you pay!"

But now the stranger leaped across the room, brandishing his staff. At its touch, the hands relaxed their cruel grip on the woman's throat. A look of

mortal anguish passed over the dead face, and the flesh began to melt away from its forehead.

Like the wax of a burning candle, it trickled from brow to cheek, from cheek to chin. It carried away with it the look of pain from the eyes, the anguish from the mouth. Slowly and inexorably, the stark, white bones of an anonymous skull took the place of the once-dear face. Like rain dripping from autumn trees, flesh fell from every finger and oozed away from the feet. The garments hung in voluminous folds, too large now for the skeleton beneath.

Then the whistle of a winter wind was heard in the chimney, and from the hearth rushed an evil form, a creature of smoke and fire, with a huge black cloak floating out from its shoulders. Reaching out with one skeletal arm, it enfolded the husband's remains in the cloak and bore them away up the chimney.

The fire died in the hearth and the room turned dark and cold. The woman kneeled on the hard stone floor, crying for mercy. The stranger heaved a sigh and lifted her to her feet. "It is not for the living to know the fate of the dead," he said. Then he opened the door, and the widow watched him walk noiselessly away through the dry leaves and vanish up the misty hillside.

·7·

Furies of the Far North

When winter came to the Arctic, the sun hid below the horizon, condemning the Inuit people to months of cold and darkness. As hunger and isolation took their toll, magic grew stronger: Invisible enemies were sensed everywhere, and people fell prey to strange cravings for the taste of human flesh. Only the shamans, masters of spells and rituals, could subdue the spirits abroad in the long night. These wizards were themselves objects of awe, needed but never trusted.

In Greenland, Inuit elders told a cautionary tale of a wizard who abused his powers. He lived apart from his tribe, in a hut by the edge of a glacier. In summer, he was guided by his spirit guardians to high, hidden meadows where great herds of caribou grazed. He passed the winters crouched by a fire that never died, listening to the voices borne on the Arctic wind. In between the two seasons, he always paid a visit to his brother, who eked out a poor living as a hunter. Warmed by these reunions, the shaman never saw the look of envy that each year burned brighter in his brother's eye.

One summer, the spirits guided the wizard farther afield than ever before. The first snowfall found him still hunting the caribou. Engrossed in the chase, he delayed his visit to his brother until the six-month darkness had begun. When he arrived, the shaman found his sibling looking drawn and haggard. In reply to the shaman's request, he said that he had lost his appetite when his brother failed to come at the appointed time. But now the feasting could begin. With glittering eyes and hysterical laughter, he produced a chunk of seal meat from a soapstone pot and invited his brother to eat.

Before the shaman could take a bite, he felt a sharp tug at the sleeve of his parka. He looked down: There was nothing. He said to his brother that he would not be so ill-bred as to eat without providing a taste of his own meat in exchange. With this excuse he stepped outside, still carrying the chunk of food. The wind rose and spit snow into his eyes. Then he heard the spirits' voices and knew that the meat was not seal but human flesh.

The shaman struggled to comprehend his brother's malice. It was well known

Of all the forms of madness that plagued the Arctic tribes, none was dreaded more than the insatiable craving for human flesh.

that the eating of even a single mouthful of human flesh engendered an insatiable appetite for more: A man became capable of killing child or parent to assuage the hunger. It had never before occurred to the wizard that his brother might resent his magic powers, or that he might be jealous of the help he received from spirits on the hunting ground. The shaman put aside the ties of blood and loyalty and planned his revenge. The brother who had tried to drive him mad would himself be cursed instead. If he had not already become a cannibal, his intended victim would turn him into one.

Taking a fine piece of caribou from his own sled, he contaminated it by rubbing it with the chunk of human meat, then threw that gobbet of forbidden flesh away. Returning inside, he wiped his mouth on his sleeve and feigned a belch of contentment. Then he fed the tainted caribou to his brother. He waited for the first symptoms of the madness to appear. When the brother looked at the shaman with a speculative expression, fondled the blade of his hunting knife and licked his lips, the wizard knew he had succeeded. He made a hurried departure.

In the course of his journey along the frozen fjord, with the huskies baying at the moon, the shaman's relief at his escape turned to remorse. At home he could neither rest nor dream, but tossed sleeplessly. Within a week, guilt drove him back to his brother's igloo.

Outside, the dogs howled, but within, all was silent. The shaman pushed his way into the passage and cautiously lifted the flap. The white walls were smeared with crimson; handprints clawed their way across the low ceiling; pools of blood congealed on the floor. Gnawed flesh and severed limbs littered the sleeping platform. The shaman's stomach heaved as he recognized the half-chewed faces of his brother's nearest neighbors.

Rearing up from a pile of hides, the killer lunged at the shaman with his knife. The shaman kicked his crazed brother away and rushed out of the igloo, ready to leap into his dogsled and bolt for safety. Maddened by the smell of fresh blood, his team of huskies were snarling and straining in their ropes.

The man-eater approached the sled and began to speak words of apology, as if his reason had suddenly been restored to him. The shaman put down his whip and silenced the dogs, but as soon as he stepped out of the sled, the cannibal attacked again. Only by paralyzing him temporarily with a powerful spell was the shaman able to escape.

In the unbroken darkness of winter, he lay awake in his stone house, and memories of childhood came back to haunt him. He entreated the spirits to undo the damage, but they were silent. Remorse drove him back to his brother once more. The igloo lay chill and empty, sheltering only the dead; the living beast that had devoured their flesh was gone. In the moonlight, the shaman saw footprints crossing the fresh snow. He followed their winding path up the hillside, and in a gully beneath a cliff he found his brother, crouching and slumped forward.

A shaman learned from the spirits that his own brother sought to trick him into tasting human meat. Outraged, he wrought a vengeance that plunged his sibling into a pit of horrors.

When the shaman touched him, he fell back, a bloated corpse whose open eyes were cups of frozen blood.

News of the tragedy spread quickly through the scattered settlements. Although his brother had tried to poison him first, it was the shaman, as survivor, who became a pariah. His people would rather suffer assaults by the spirits than contaminate themselves by contact with a fratricide. In the end he went mad. Every morsel of food he touched seemed to be tainted with the stench of rotting human flesh. Every drop of water tasted of blood or bile. He was not seen in the settlements for many months, and when people finally went in search of him, they found him dead on the floor of his hut, surrounded by piles of rotting meat.

His was a cautionary tale, a reminder that even a shaman could be caught in the meshes of evil. But the Arctic lore was far richer in accounts of wizards who succeeded in vanquishing the dark forces.

The tribal bards told of a confrontation with a being that was neither ghost nor human. It began on an afternoon at the end of winter, when a man half mad with terror came to beg a shaman's help. His family was being persecuted. Whenever he and his brothers went out in their kayaks, the calm waters of the inlet became so agitated that the ice floes grated against one another and the canoes were nearly capsized. He had only glimpsed the enemy from a distance: something small but powerful, darting across the ice at incredible speed.

The shaman pondered for a moment, then asked if any newborn infant had been left out to die. The man admitted that his unmarried sister had given birth to a girl-child earlier that winter. The family had been on the verge of starvation; they had barely enough to feed themselves, let alone a small, unwelcome stranger. The brothers had taken the baby from its mother, filled its mouth with snow, and had left the small body in the wilderness.

The wizard inquired if the baby had been given a name before it was abandoned. The man replied that it had, and the shaman hissed his disapproval. He told them that by destroying an infant who had acquired a name, and therefore a soul, they had created an *angiak*, a child of the living dead. The flesh of such an infant might decay, but its spirit would live on, seeking revenge.

Questioned further, the man revealed that he had sometimes been wakened in the night and thought himself dreaming, for he saw a child that was not quite human nuzzling at his sister's breast. This was to be expected, said the wizard. An *angiak* needed sustenance: Every night, it returned to its mother to suck out strength enough to continue its vendetta.

The shaman harnessed his dogs to the sled and followed the man down the coast to his home village. As they sped along the shore, they could see the dark shapes of the icebergs casting ghostly shadows across the water. The entire population of the village was on the beach, watching two men in kayaks struggling toward the shore. Bearing down on them was the *angiak*—its kayak was the upended skull of

Victims of infanticide lingered on earth in a living death. Their angry spirits, known as angiaks, stole home at night to the nourishment from their mother's breasts, until they gathered sufficient strength to punish those who had murdered them.

a dog, its paddle a canine leg bone. At the creature's approach, the waters spiraled into a massive whirlpool. The kayaks and the screaming men were sucked into its vortex. A squeal of inhuman laughter reverberated off the rocks, but the *angiak* was nowhere to be found.

The crowd rushed forward to attempt a rescue. Fishing hooks fastened to lines, they trolled back and forth and finally managed to pull up one of the victims. As he came to the surface, the water froze, encasing him in ice—mouth agape, eyes wide, caught in the moment of his death.

The shaman did not wait for the recovery of the second body. He turned his face to the horizon and entreated the spirits' help. The woman who had borne the *angiak* began to moan, and the shaman felt the sharp tug of an invisible hand on his sleeve. A strange voice, belonging to some mighty spirit of the tundra, came from within him. It roared out the name of the murdered child, and commanded it to leave the land of the living.

With a rattle of bones the *angiak* emerged from the ice floes and, growing ever smaller, paddled frantically out toward the open sea. Caught in the returning sun's first rays, the tiny speck seemed to burst into flame, emitted a dying screech, and disappeared beneath the waves. Weak from his exertions, the shaman returned to the wilderness. He had vanquished one demon, but knew that a thousand more would spring up in its place, for the seed of evil rode the wailing Arctic winds.

Spying the kayaks bearing the uncles who had killed it, the angiak stirred the bay into a maelstrom that sucked the men to a death of agony under the ice floes.

·8·

Bloodguilt of a Royal House

Beneath its brilliant Aegean skies, the land of Greece was the scene of many horrors: bacchanalian orgies of rape, death and human sacrifice. But no tale of the ancient poets was so bloodsoaked as that curse that fell upon the noble House of Atreus: a malignity that, once conjured into being, thrived for generations, spawning madness, despair and obscenities beyond imagining.

It began many thousands of years ago, at a time when the gods regularly intervened in the lives of mortals. A warrior-prince called Pelops resolved to bid for the hand of Hippodameia, daughter of King Oenomaus of Elis. It was the old man's custom to challenge every suitor to a chariot race. He decreed that if the contender triumphed, he would win both the daughter's hand and the crown of Elis; but should the aspirant fail, he would immediately forfeit his life.

People whispered that Oenomaus persisted in this game because he himself had conceived an incestuous passion for his beautiful daughter and wished to prevent her marrying. Whether that was so or not, there seemed no possibility that he would ever lose a race: His horses, gifts of the war-god Ares, were children of the wind; his charioteer, Myrtilus, was son to Hermes—winged messenger of the gods. Every suitor, even when granted a half hour's start, was overtaken at the last moment by the maniacally laughing King and speared through like a stuck pig. As a warning to prospective bridegrooms, Oenomaus impaled the skulls of his defeated rivals on spikes around the arched doorway of the palace.

But before Pelops went to Elis, he sought divine aid of his own, praying to Poseidon, lord of the oceans. The sea-god sent him a magnificent winged chariot and a team of immortal horses—beasts so swift they could gallop over water as well as land. Pelops drove this vehicle to the palace of King Oenomaus, dismounted and stood before the archway, staring up at the grim skulls. Then he plunged through the entrance into darkness.

Groping his way through the gloom of a long corridor, Pelops suddenly felt strong fingers grasp his wrist. The haggard face of Myrtilus loomed in the dark and studied him closely. The charioteer

Suitors to the King of Elis' daughter were forced to compete against the monarch in a
chariot race. The prize for victory was the Princess; the price of failure was the loser's life.
An archway built of prospective bridegrooms' skulls stood before the palace as a warning.

spoke: He himself was ablaze with lust for Hippodameia. If he ensured that his master lost the race, would Pelops give him the woman for the wedding night? The crushing grip tightened. Slowly, Pelops nodded. In this way the first seeds of treachery were sown, for Pelops did not intend to let Myrtilus remain alive once he had served his purpose.

The charioteer, for his part, kept faith. He sabotaged the axles of his master's chariot, and persuaded Oenomaus to drive alone. The ensuing race was closely run: The teams strained neck and neck to pass one another, until at last Oenomaus bellowed in frustration and grabbed his spear. Even as he aimed at Pelops' dancing back, the wheels catapulted away from his chariot, and—because the reins were bound tightly around his forearms—he was thrown from the platform and dragged screaming and flailing across the ground. By the time the horses finally stopped, Oenomaus was dead.

Pelops, finishing the circular course in triumph, drew in his chariot to collect both collaborator and prize. Then the trio sped across the sea to the island of Euboea, their chariot clipping the crests of the waves like a flying fish. As they neared their destination, Myrtilus called to the young King, reminding him of the bargain they had struck. Smiling assent, Pelops suddenly dealt the charioteer a savage blow that sent him tumbling from the chariot and into the sea. Myrtilus thrashed in the water and watched his betrayer disappear over the horizon. As he felt the sea invade his lungs, he laid a curse on Pelops and all his children.

The god Hermes heard the utterance of his drowning son and took it upon himself to ensure that the curse bore fruit. Pelops, harrowed in dreams by guilty remembrance of his crime, strove to make his peace with Myrtilus' divine father, dedicating glorious temples to his name.

But Hermes was not appeased. In the second generation, the curse erupted in the rivalry between two sons of Pelops—Atreus and Thyestes. Both Princes were candidates for the throne of the wealthy kingdom of Mycenae, whose old monarch was dying without an heir. An oracle had warned the Mycenaeans that they must choose his successor from the family of Pelops, and so the two brothers traveled to the city to compete for the crown. Hermes watched their growing enmity and diligently nourished it. Under his guidance, Aerope, Atreus' new wife, fell desperately in

Thyestes seduced the wife of Atreus, but the cuckold took revenge. He slew Thyestes' children, bade their unwitting father to a banquet and served up their dismembered corpses as the climax of the feast.

love with Thyestes, who proceeded to cuckold his brother. Even as he exchanged secret caresses with Aerope, Thyestes pondered how to manipulate this liaison to secure himself the throne. But quite the opposite occurred: Atreus discovered the adultery. Where another betrayed husband would have drawn his sword in fury, he, by a judicious public exhibition of sorrow and forgiveness, won both the respect of the elders and the Mycenaean crown. Aerope, repentant, became his Queen, and Thyestes, exposed as a cynic and a deceiver, slunk away to lick his wounds.

But the shame of cuckoldry festered in Atreus' soul. For years thereafter, he nursed a hatred for Thyestes. The imagined picture of those sallow fingers running over his wife's body grew more detailed and unendurable as time went by. At last, he devised a scheme for reprisal. In a gesture of fraternal reconciliation, he invited Thyestes to a banquet to celebrate the rebirth of their friendship

and love. Thyestes, wary but curious, accepted. But even as the brothers embraced and kissed, assassins stole into the chambers where Thyestes' five young sons were sleeping and slit their throats.

Ignorant of the carnage, Thyestes that night gorged himself from a great platter of sauced and garnished meat. He had little conversation for his dull brother, but when his belly was stretched tight as a drum, Thyestes asked the name of the dish he had enjoyed so much. In answer, Atreus himself brought forward a large covered salver and plucked off the lid. There lay the hacked-off heads, hands, feet—every identifiable piece of Thyestes' sons. Thyestes flung himself to the ground in a frenzy; his bowels convulsed in riot, and from his mouth and nose the half-digested flesh and viscera of his children vomited in an obscene torrent. Through tears of rage, he cursed his brother by all the evils in the world, then crawled away to plan his revenge.

Before taking any action, he went to consult the great Oracle at Delphi.

There, Thyestes learned that, to combat Atreus, he must sire a child by his own daughter, the priestess Pelopia. Only a boy born of such a union could avenge the monstrous slaughter of his children. At this news, Thyestes hung his head in sorrow. Evil was breeding evil.

Nevertheless, he rode to the temple where Pelopia served, and waited unseen in the woods nearby until she came to wash at the stream. As she stepped into the cover of the trees, Thyestes fell upon his daughter, pushed her face into the ground so that she might not recognize him, and raped her. In fighting to protect herself, Pelopia managed to grab her attacker's sword, and held tightly to it until he had finished and run off. Henceforth she kept it with her always, determined someday to identify its owner.

Atreus, too, consulted the Oracle at Delphi and was told to find his brother. From Delphi he followed his trail to the temple, where he found Pelopia sitting on the steps, keening in her misery. Hermes, divine messenger and implacable enemy of Atreus' line, had brought the two together and now molded their destinies to suit his plans for revenge.

Under his invisible influence Atreus fell in love with Pelopia, his own niece, and, abandoning his search for Thyestes, took her for his wife. He was free to do so: Before leaving Mycenae he had ordered Aerope's execution.

In time, Pelopia bore the child her father had planted in her womb. Loathing it as the fruit of rape, she tried to murder the boy—abandoning him on a mountainside. Atreus, however, retrieved him, named him Aegisthus and raised him as his heir. But his agents continued to search for his brother. When Thyestes was at last tracked down and forcibly brought to Mycenae, Atreus flung him into a dungeon. He then commanded Aegisthus, who was just seven years old, to prove his manhood by going down alone and killing the prisoner.

Terrified of failing the test, the boy stole to his mother's room and took from under her bed the sword she kept hidden there. He crept down the stone steps to the filthy cell where the victim lay sleeping. For a long time, he stood looking at the man, his blade raised and wavering, again and again putting off the blow.

Suddenly Thyestes sat up and grabbed the boy's arm, ripping the sword from his grasp. Aegisthus screamed, and at once his mouth was stifled by a hand. Where, demanded the prisoner, did he find the sword? Released, Aegisthus tearfully explained. To his alarm, Thyestes flung back his head and laughed like a jackal, then viciously gripped the boy and shook him again. He would, he hissed, spare Aegisthus' life if he performed three services. The first was to fetch Pelopia to the dungeon immediately. Babbling with gratitude, Aegisthus fled back to the palace and furtively sought out his mother.

When Pelopia came, she instantly recognized her father and fell into his arms. Thyestes stroked his daughter's hair and thanked her for returning his long-lost sword to him. Pulling away to see her father's face, and suddenly understanding his words, Pelopia snatched the blade and rammed it into her own heart. Thyestes watched impassively, then slowly drew the weapon free. He turned once more to Aegisthus, who crouched whimpering in a corner, and told the boy how to perform his next service. He must bear the blood-smeared sword to Atreus and pronounce his duty done, then as quickly as possible return below. The boy obeyed.

When he heard that Thyestes had been disposed of, a great weight rolled from Atreus' mind. Proudly lifting his son into the air, he proclaimed the day a feast day and ordered his slaves to bring him wine. In the dungeon, while the court feasted, Aegisthus learned the true identity of Thyestes and the story of his own conception. Like a hardened assassin, the small boy climbed slowly up to the palace to perform his third service: to avenge the atrocity his real father had sustained at Atreus' hands.

While Atreus lolled in a drunken stupor, Aegisthus sprang on him and hacked him to death. So it was that Thyestes avenged the death of his sons and succeeded to the throne of Mycenae.

But the curse spread to the third generation. When their father perished, Agamemnon and Menelaus, sons of Atreus by the dead Aerope, fled the court. The young Princes roamed the Aegean, eking out a perilous living as mercenaries. Finally, they won the patronage of warlike Tyndareus, King of Sparta. With his help, Agamemnon stormed Mycenae and deposed Thyestes. Aegisthus, too, fled

for his life, but the paths of the step-brothers were again to cross.

Some years later, war exploded upon the Greek world. Paris, son of Priam, the Trojan King, kidnapped Menelaus' beautiful wife, Helen, and sailed off to Troy with her. Honor had been flouted, and Agamemnon resolved, as head of the family, to take the woman back by force. He therefore launched a massive expeditionary fleet against the city of Troy.

After he left, Aegisthus, grown to manhood, crept out from hiding. Returning to Mycenae, he insinuated himself once more into the court—now presided over by Clytemnestra, the lonely wife of Agamemnon. Without even attempting to disguise himself, Aegisthus sought to seduce her. She, for her part, had little reason to love her husband: She had married Agamemnon only under duress. Yet she steadfastly repelled Aegisthus' advances, until a day when heralds from the army brought her terrible news.

The gods, foreseeing dreadful carnage for a cause they considered dubious, had marooned the Greek fleet at Aulis, far from Troy. They then presented Agamemnon with a choice: He could turn back, or—if he wished to persevere—he would first have to summon his beloved daughter Iphigenia to Aulis and offer her up as a sacrifice. He struggled to choose between his duty as a father and his obligation as leader of his men. In the privacy of his pavilion, Agamemnon paced for hours, wrestling with his conscience. Then he acted. The girl was sent for.

When he lied to Iphigenia that she had been brought to the altar dressed in white because she was to marry a hero, the blood burned in his face for shame; when he signaled the priests to stab her, he wept like a baby. But tears and sorrow could not excuse Agamemnon, least of all to his wife. For sacrificing their daughter in the name of expedience, Clytemnestra punished her spouse with the first means at hand. She embraced Aegisthus with a passion fired by loathing of her husband. Above all, she longed for Agamemnon to return alive: The murder she planned for him would eclipse the whole history of horror in their accursed family.

After ten long years, Troy fell and Agamemnon returned to Mycenae. Clytemnestra greeted him with outstretched arms. Taking his hand, she led him to the bathhouse and lovingly undressed him. Then she struck. Trapping her victim's head in a thick towel and forcing it backward, she shrieked out to Aegisthus, lying in wait nearby. Aegisthus leaped from his hiding-place and plunged a dagger into his stepbrother again and again, until all were soaked in gore. But Agamemnon was strong: He would not die. Finally Clytemnestra seized an ax and struck off his head.

Aegisthus slid to the floor, exhausted; but Clytemnestra was not finished. Ax in hand, she searched for her own children, desperate to do away with her son. If she did not, he would grow up to avenge his father's death by murdering her. Knowing what would be in her mother's mind, Electra sent her young brother Orestes into hiding. She returned to the palace at nightfall, a living reminder that Agamemnon's line still survived. She was determined to denounce the killers, even at the cost of her own life. Aegisthus had drawn his sword to cut her down, but Clytemnestra restrained him, pointing out that as a girl she posed no threat— vengeance was the work of sons. Thereafter Electra remained precariously but conspicuously alive at Mycenae, every day haranguing the people with the fact of their rulers' shameful crime. Because the citizens feared Clytemnestra's anger, they pretended that her daughter's tirades were the rantings of a mad woman.

Clytemnestra, however, lived in fear of her son. She knew that no matter how long he had to wait, Orestes would one day come for her. He waited twenty years, but he surely came. And the night before he found her, Clytemnestra had a nightmare. She dreamed of giving birth to a hideous snake. She suckled it, and it drew black blood from her breast. Screaming, she struggled to wrench it away, but its jaws were tightly clamped. Clytemnestra woke sweating in the dark and knew that she was about to die.

Even as she drew the sheets about her and moaned in fear, Orestes was approaching Mycenae. Ever since going into exile, he had yearned for the moment when he could feel Clytemnestra's blood flow over his hands; and now the Delphic Oracle had deemed the time propitious for just vengeance.

Every morning, Electra came out of the city to the scrubland where Agamemnon lay buried, there to remember her father. When she saw a man waiting for

Clytemnestra, Queen of Agamemnon, helped her lover to murder her royal spouse. She dreamed that she bore and suckled a poisonous snake, and knew what the nightmare portended. Her children would avenge their father's death and show her no mercy.

His hands incarnadined with his mother's blood, Orestes, son of Clytemnestra, fled the Furies' wrath. But these immortal avengers tracked him down and hounded him to madness.

her in the gray dawn, she recognized Orestes at once and ran to embrace him. Seeing a weapon in his hand, she told him of Clytemnestra's nightmare—for the woman's screams had woken the whole palace. Orestes nodded: He was the serpent his mother had suckled.

Electra led her brother to the palace, where he called out to Clytemnestra, saying he brought news from a foreign land that her son Orestes was dead. Clytemnestra's heart danced at the words. Bounding down the stairs from her bedchamber, she shouted to Aegisthus to open the door. Her lover, bleary with sleep, drew the bolts.

Orestes crashed in. Without a word, he drove his knife into Aegisthus' mouth and out through the back of his head. Next he turned to Clytemnestra. Although she begged him to be merciful, Orestes seized his mother by the hair, dragged her to the corpse of her lover and slit her throat. Then he made a great mistake. Glancing up to the top of the stairs, he saw the small daughter of Aegisthus and Clytemnestra looking down in terror. Chasing her to her chamber, Orestes held the little girl to the wall and slashed her to death with his knife.

By now a rabble of curious citizens was clamoring at the palace gate. Breathless, Orestes spoke to them in the courtyard. Had he not done right, he asked, to purge Mycenae of its evil tyrants? Had not the gods themselves condoned their execution? The crowd seemed satisfied, but the gods were not. No justification for the brutal slaughter of the child could be claimed in their name. Even as Orestes

spoke, the Furies—merciless agents of the gods' anger—dived down from a seemingly empty blue sky and fell upon him. They seemed fashioned from nightmare, with vipers for hair, the faces of dogs, and the cowled, skeletal wings of bats. For six days and nights, the screeching beasts clawed and gouged at Orestes' flesh, taking care not to kill him but inflicting all the pain that a mortal could possibly withstand. Then, inexplicably, the vile creatures left him.

Orestes staggered from the palace to the marketplace, where the people had gathered to seek the wisdom of the gods. The finest animals had been sacrificed, libations of wine poured into the thirsty earth, incense floated on the wind. Finally the answer came. The wisest of the priests decreed that Orestes had no license from the gods and should be cast out for his crimes, never to be granted water, food or shelter by any Mycenaean.

So it happened that Orestes was flung out by the very city he had liberated. For a year he wandered the barren lands around Mycenae, pursued at every turn by the Furies, eating only bark and mud and the lice from his own skin. For a whole year he could not wash the blood of his victims from his hands. Madness began to gnaw at Orestes—until at last Athena, compassionate goddess of law and reason, absolved him of his crimes, healed him and let him live again in peace. Her divine intervention eradicated the curse that for four generations had tortured the House of Atreus.

·9·

A Stormy Reckoning

In the dark fjords of northern Norway, the fishermen of old knew well that the world harbored much greater dangers than the caprices of the sea. Pitching on a leaden swell, waiting for fish to find their nets, they would frighten one another with tales of folk who had encountered other-worldly perils and had paid the price—tales of men like the fisherman Elias, who one day damned himself and his family because his belly was empty and his pride was great.

Elias' fault was to spear a seal stranded on the shore near his home. Like all seafarers of the northern coasts, he knew the beasts to be unlucky; it was said they housed the souls of sinners who had drowned themselves. Caution told him to leave well alone. But he had six children to feed, and they had tasted no meat for a month. Running forward, he thrust his harpoon into the beast's back.

With unnatural force the seal writhed free, breaking the weapon in two, and pulled itself upright. For a split second, Elias found himself looking into eyes that burned and at a mouth twisted with hatred. Then the beast was gone. Only the splintered shaft of the harpoon remained, rolling back and forth in the surf.

The months passed and Elias soon forgot the incident. Each day he sailed out with the tide; each night he worked in the boat house, keeping his vessel clean and seaworthy. It was there that he had his first premonition of troubles to come. As he crouched over the upturned hull one evening, he glanced up to see the face of a stranger, grinning maniacally, inches before his eyes. He leaped up, upsetting the hurricane lamp and sending shadows wheeling across the rafters. A moment later the visitor was gone, but not before Elias had caught a glimpse of the iron spike that

utted from his back. Elias told no one of what he had seen. He knew what they would say: that he was in thrall to a *draug*—one of a race of malevolent spirits that were said to rise from the sea to stalk mortals singled out for death. Nobody would sail with a man marked out by a *draug*, nor buy his fish. Such a one was accursed.

Elias went about his trade cautiously in the weeks that followed, hugging the coastline like a novice in his single-masted skiff. He knew that if the stranger in the shed had come to haunt him, the boat itself could no longer be trusted; one touch of those ghoulish fingers could warp even the stoutest timbers. For a month or more, nothing untoward happened. Then one afternoon, Elias hauled in his nets to discover that they were full of a reeking foam. He recoiled in disgust and something like despair, for he recognized the flecked and stinking froth to be the vomit of a *draug*, an omen of death by drowning.

Hearing the approach of another craft, Elias dropped the nets back into the water to hide their contents.. As he did so, a voice boomed across the swell, calling out his name. Yet when he turned to reply to the other boatman, he found himself staring at empty ocean. As far as the horizon there was no other vessel in sight.

For some weeks afterward, Elias took to his bed, feigning sickness as an excuse for not putting out to sea. But food ran short, and the sight of his family wasting with hunger finally forced him to master his fears and face the waters once more. He soon came to believe all his apprehensions unfounded: His catches were large, and there was no sign of the *draug*. In time, Elias decided that the shadow over him must have lifted, and he dismissed the matter entirely from his mind.

Eight years passed. His eldest son, Bernt, reached adolescence and soon was old enough to accompany his father on the daily fishing run. With the extra help, Elias found that he could stay out at sea longer, and his catch increased greatly as a result. The family ate well and still managed to put money aside. The day came when there was enough for Elias to buy a new boat.

One December morning, he set off with his wife and children for the port of Rangen, where the finest boat-builder of the district lived. He told him of his needs, and the old man duly uncovered a sturdy five-hander he had tarred over that very fall. Elias appraised it critically and liked what he saw; the boat was a craftsman's masterpiece, built not just to endure

After years of thrift and toil, Elias saved silver enough to afford a better boat.
His wife and children joined him on the old vessel's last
journey, a winter excursion to the nearest port, to purchase the new craft.

means, he closed the deal on the spot. Then he led his excited family down the quayside steps to take possession and sail the vessel home.

With eight aboard and baskets of Christmas provisions besides, the boat lay heavy in the water at first. But as soon as she nosed out of the seawall's sanctuary and into open water, her mainsail billowed with a crack. She lifted her bows to the air and sped across the waves, clipping their crests like a skimming pebble.

Elias, who was laughing aloud with joy, cried out to his family that their new boat must surely be the fastest on the whole coast. No sooner had the words left his mouth, though, than he noticed another craft, identical in design, bucking past them on a parallel tack. Squinting through the thin drizzle that had begun to whip out of the sky, Elias could just see the backs of the crew, who appeared to be leaning out against the swell. They were racing him.

Suddenly, all the good judgment acquired in a lifetime of sailing deserted the fisherman. He could see that the weather was worsening. The leaden gloom that every sailor loathes had come to squat over the sea; a vicious squall was about to break. Good sense told him to head promptly for home. But his pride was at stake. Over the rising wind, he shouted to his son Bernt to loosen the clews holding the sail steady. Unleashed, the craft surged forward, hurdling the deepening troughs and dousing the family with spray.

As night began to tumble down, the twin vessels raced on, side by side. Elias marveled at the phosphorescent sea fire that crackled and foamed about the other boat. Who were these men? Unsummoned, an ugly memory stirred in the fisherman's mind.

Suddenly anxious, Elias was filled with a concern for his family, silent now and huddled together in the pitching boat. He signaled urgently to Bernt to make fast the clews and set the vessel at a safer angle to the wind. But his instruction came too late. At that very moment, a mountainous roller exploded upon them from above, so unexpectedly that it seemed to fall from out of the sky. As the crashing water filled his mouth and ears, Elias thought he heard a cry; when the wave had subsided, he found that it was his wife who was screaming. The two youngest children, whom she had been clutching tightly to her side, had been torn from her arms and swept over the side of the boat.

Elias felt the nausea of despair. The storm made it impossible to turn back for the lost children. As he sought some shards of hope, a second

*Homeward bound in the midst of a gale, Elias was impelled
to race with a boatload of strangers. The challengers' craft was twin to
his own, save for the inexplicable glow it cast upon the water.*

wave loomed out of the darkness. Elias laid the prow aslant to it and bellowed at Bernt to open the sail, but his words were swamped as the groaning vessel was once more engulfed. The fisherman felt a body flung against his own and grabbed for it, but it was ripped from his grasp. Through a riot of white water his eyes met his wife's as, with arms outstretched and flailing, she was borne high up in the air on the lip of the wave, and out into the blackness.

Just then, as Elias gazed uncomprehendingly down the boat at the remnants of his family, the vessel that had been racing them ducked close alongside. The man at the tiller seemed relaxed, even nonchalant, in the face of the terrible storm. He turned toward Elias and tapped the side of his nose conspiratorially. Then he pulled the boat sharply away, out into the night. Only a glint of moonlight on metal protruding from his back showed where he had gone.

Another wave rose up in a sheer cliff. Bernt shouted a warning, but it was upon them before Elias could move. The craft was smashed downward, then surfaced with its keel in the air. Elias clung to the rudder, Bernt and one other son, Martin, clasped the oarlocks. The others were gone. Elias bade the survivors hold on tight and keep their courage; there was nothing else they could do.

They drifted for an hour or so, and the wind dropped. Elias heard a voice from the far side of the upturned boat. It was Bernt, saying that Martin was dead. A snicker of laughter rippled across the dark swell. Looking over his shoulder, the fisherman saw the other vessel, sailing close by once more. Finally he understood what he must do in order to save the life of his remaining son. It was only through his own death, long ago ordained, that the *draug* would be placated.

And so it was that, far out in the Arctic wastes of the ocean, Bernt learned from his father's lips the full story of his fateful meeting with the *draug*. Elias told him all. Then, his explanation finished, the fisherman let go his grasp and sank, without protest, down into the depths. He opened his mouth to the ocean; and all around him, as the liquid fingers of death closed about his lungs, the sounds of a deep, aquatic laughter filled his ears.

They found Bernt, delirious with cold and fear, the following morning on the rocks offshore. As his rescuers wrapped blankets about him, the boy jabbered of spells and curses and pointed wildly out toward the deep. But all they could see was a bull seal, circling lazily near the shore.

Capsized and engulfed by massive waves, only Elias and his eldest son survived. But the sea stayed angry, demanding one final sacrifice.

·10·

Bride of the Ghost-Chief

In centuries past, the Indians who lived on the fogbound western coast of North America would sit before their longhouses in the evenings, straining their ears to catch a sound from the land of the dead. It lay across the water but close by, the shamans said, and there had been a time when the living could journey there. With the aging of the world, however, the border between real and magical, living and dead, had closed. Now only a single creature could move freely between the two realms. That was the screech owl, and whenever people saw it pass overhead or heard its almost human cry, they shuddered to think of the place from which it came.

A tale of earlier days told of the last human to visit that strange land. She was a young woman, the daughter of a great chief. The house in which she lived was the wealthiest in the village. A magnificent totem stood before it to inform visitors of the many mythical animals the family counted among their ancestors. The girl was beautiful, and many young men sought her for their bride. Her father wanted her company for himself,

however; having no need of the bride price, he refused them all.

The young woman hid her sadness, but her suitors did not conceal their anger. The chief's refusals were seen as a sign of arrogance and contempt. People said he would be punished for his pride.

They were soon proved right. The chief was rash enough to reject the son of the tribal shaman, a man renowned for his understanding of the spirit world. His family dishonored, the shaman sought a magical implement potent enough to punish the chief. He made his way to a cave in the forest, a place of mystery and spiritual power where quartz crystals glittered in the gloom. Cradling a loose fragment of the rock in his palm, he intoned a chant in time to the vibrations he felt from the mighty stones around him, asking the spirit people to take the chief's daughter as their bride.

That night, the daughter was drawn from her longhouse by the sound of singing voices approaching across the water. Torches of pitchwood gleamed in the darkness; many canoes were coming toward the village. She saw that it was a

Guided by torchlight, the canoes of a wedding party brought a bridegroom from a strange country across the bay to bid for the hand of a chieftain's daughter.

wedding party, for the boats were piled high with costly gifts. And when a handsome young chieftain stepped from the first canoe and touched her hand, she realized that she was the intended bride. She did not notice the shaman, who was standing close by on the beach, smiling impassively to himself.

The visitor ordered his people to unload the canoes and carry the presents into the longhouse. The bride price he was offering far exceeded any that the village had ever seen. Piles of blankets were brought in, woven of the hair of mountain goats and the strong fiber of red cedar. Intricately carved boxes, upon which mystic creatures danced with their mouths leering wide, came next, followed by carved stone pipes, disks of polished abalone, masks decorated with beads and hair, and spruce-root baskets woven so tightly that they could hold water. Finally the suitor himself made his entrance, preceded by the rarest treasures of all: shining shields of precious copper from the far north, each worth many hundreds of blankets.

The girl could see her father was impressed by the young chief's munificence, as well as by his polite and respectful demeanor. He let himself be won over. To her silent joy, he gave his permission for her to be married to the stranger.

A wedding feast was soon prepared, at which the villagers sang of past glories and of the exploits of their tribal ancestors. After the marriage rituals had been completed, the visitors and the smiling bride climbed into the canoes and disappeared into the night.

The journey seemed to take only moments, and when they arrived at their destination it was still dark. Despite the late hour, the chieftain's village was full of people. The bride was greeted from all sides by happy, smiling crowds. She was led by her husband to the most splendid longhouse she had ever seen. Even in the darkness, she could tell that it was larger and finer than her father's, containing the sleeping quarters of a dozen or more families. She was proud to find that the clan she had married into was so rich and numerous, and happier still that her husband was so ardent and strong.

The marriage night was long and passionate, but finally she fell asleep, nestling close to her groom on the soft skins that formed their bed. But her mind was troubled, and dark phantoms assailed her rest. Trapped in the border zone between sleeping and waking, she stirred fitfully through what remained of the night.

When she finally came full awake, a pale light filtered through the chinks in the wall-beams. A stench of singed hair and burning flesh filled the longhouse, and the world was wrapped in a strange, frightening silence. She turned for reassurance to the man lying beside her. As she touched him, her unease congealed into horror. Her fingers had fallen not on taut skin and firm muscle but on something cold and moist. The young man she had married was gone. In his place lay a cadaver in the last stages of decay.

She jerked her hand away. As she did so, she disturbed the skull, which fell

On the morning after her nuptials, the bride awoke to find herself embracing a skeleton. The air around her marriage bed was heavy with smoke and the odor of decomposing flesh.

sideways, turning its eye-sockets toward her. At that, the girl fled through the house and out into the hazy sunlight, only to find the shore littered with countless more bones. The happy people of the previous night had all disappeared; now she was the lone survivor in an ossuary. Sobbing, she ran to the edge of the water and out into the waves.

The cold waters of the bay calmed her. Realizing she had not been followed, she tried to think of some way that she could escape. At once she remembered the canoes that had borne her from her home. She waded back to the shore and hurried to the place where they were moored. There she found that the stout vessels of the night before had become useless, rotting hulls, coated with seaweed and awash to their gunwales.

But she did not yet despair, for she had seen a wisp of smoke rising from the next cove. Here at last was a sign of life, and she plunged toward it, no longer noticing if she stepped on or scattered the piles of human bones. The maker of the fire proved to be a stoutly built old woman. She ran to her, blurting out questions.

Stumbling over human bones, the bride fled to the beach.
But the gaily painted canoes that had conveyed her to her
new home were nothing but half-sunken, rotting hulks.

But when the stranger told her that her name was Screech Owl, the girl's last hope was crushed. She now knew what she had already begun to suspect: She was in the land of the dead, for Screech Owl—sometimes a bird, sometimes a woman—was a spirit.

Screech Owl explained to her the ways of the land in which she was condemned to stay. Each night, she said, its inhabitants took on flesh and behaved as they had done when they were living. But at dawn, they fell where they stood, regaining their true forms as lifeless skeletons.

The old woman assured the girl that she could be happy in her new home if she would train herself to sleep during the hours of daylight, waking only at night when supple skin and tender flesh covered her companions once more.

Twilight soon fell, and with the darkness came the murmuring of the awakened dead. The sounds were not the happy ones of the night before, but groans and cries. Frightened, the girl huddled beside Screech Owl as misshapen figures loomed near, some lacking legs and arms, others with bodies that were

Maimed and battered, the people of the ghost
tribe rose up and pointed accusatory fingers
at the stranger who had come among them.

twisted and broken. All accused the girl of causing their deformities by trampling their bones as she ran along the beach. Where she had carelessly knocked aside a skull, the moonlight picked out a headless corpse; where she had crushed the delicate bones of a woman's arm underfoot, the survivor cradled a mangled limb.

Screech Owl told them that they had brought their misfortunes upon themselves by failing to explain to the bride how she must live in her new home. Muttering, the ghosts made their way back to their longhouses. The young woman returned to her husband. He too had been maimed. When she had jerked away her arm that morning, she had twisted his neck and almost severed it.

Time healed the wounds, though, and in its course the girl gradually learned how to live with her strange hosts. By remembering to keep her eyes closed until she heard her husband's voice, she never again woke next to a dead man. Through care and patience, as Screech Owl had predicted, she even came to know happiness in that strange world.

Eventually she found herself to be with child. But when she gave birth to a healthy young son, gloom spread through the village. The spirits said that the child was a living being, and could have no place in their world. Sadly, the ghost-husband told his wife that she and her offspring would have to return to her father's home.

On the fourth day after the boy's birth, the village shaman bathed him in the waters of the bay to make him strong and hardy. To the shaking of rattles and the beating of drums, he lifted the baby to the sky, commending him to the tribe's totem animal, the bear. Then he sang a sacred incantation over strips of bark from the cedar and swaddled the infant securely within them, placing him in a beautifully carved cradle. The shaman instructed the baby's mother not to unwrap the child until he had passed a full twelve days in the world of the living. If he were exposed before that time, he would become, like his father, a ghost, and would have to return, to dwell in the land of the dead forever.

When the canoes had been loaded with gifts for the girl's tribe, the group set off once more to the other world across the water. There the girl was greeted with great joy by her parents and family. Gifts were exchanged between the two tribes, their braves joined together in songs of valor and the feasting continued late into the night. Then, looking fondly on his wife and their son for the last time, the husband departed from the village with his companions. Their boats were soon lost in the darkness.

The girl waited on the shore until the sound of their singing could no longer be heard before telling her family that her husband and his people were ghosts. The tribal elders nodded at this; such things were known to happen in their day. They studied the infant she had brought back with her, remarking on how much like one of their own children he seemed. The young woman explained that he would indeed be completely human at the

Removed from its swaddling before the time was ripe, the child of the girl who married a ghost proved to be no living infant, but an unfleshed set of tiny human bones.

end of twelve days, if she heeded the warnings of the shaman.

Every morning she went out to gather thick green mosses to line the inside of his cradle, leaving her own mother to care for the baby. The woman spent the time staring into the child's face. The infant stared back at her, an unfathomable expression in his black eyes.

With each day that passed, the grandmother's curiosity grew, until she could no longer contain it. On the eleventh day, the young woman arrived home to catch the grandmother in the act of undoing the baby's wrappings. It was too late to stop her; the damage had been done. Beneath a blanket lined with the skins of the tomtit and the hummingbird lay a pattern of tiny, bleached bones resting on a layer of fine dust. The grandmother met her daughter's stricken gaze. Then, sick with guilt, she took the cradle and its grisly contents and threw it from the longhouse.

Seeing the remains of her child strewn on the ground, the young woman knew what she must do. Her baby could never now join the living; the two of them would have to return to her husband's domain. She picked up the little bones and returned them to the cradle, re-forming the body of her child so that he would be whole when restored to the ghost world. Then she squatted before the longhouse, gazing out to sea, while all around her the tribe mourned her loss.

The ghosts came for her that night. Their approach was heralded this time not by singing, but by the sound of boards being beaten, a chill rhythm signifying a death. Few words were spoken when the visitors reached the shore, and no gifts were given. The woman had only time to murmur a brief farewell to her grieving parents before the canoes slid out into the sound and she was gone.

From that day forth, contact between the two lands ceased. Some elders claimed that the girl kept the tribes apart, in retribution for her mother's folly. Others thought it was the will of the ghosts, who had revealed more of their secrets than they wished by letting her return. Whatever the reason, their canoes never again landed by the village. Over the ensuing years, however, keen-eyed young warriors would sometimes claim to have caught sight, on clear nights, of a single boat silhouetted against the moonlit waters far out in the bay. Its lone occupant sat erect and unmoving, gazing steadily toward the village. And if the wind was still, the young men said, you could often hear, above the lapping of the waves, a woman gently weeping.

·II·

The Kiss of Evil

ccording to tales of ancient days, the lands of Mesopotamia were once saturated with magic and populated with strange spirits. The desert was the home of giant birds whose huge wings could eclipse the sun, cannibal women who made their home beneath the burning sands, and others too hideous to name.

But the most numerous of the spirits of evil were the jinn. Older than humankind, they controlled the dark nights, the underground places, the wastelands and dried-up riverbeds. In their care lay the gold of long-dead tyrants, heaps of stolen treasure, all mottled and stained with blood. Mortals, made desperate by hunger or avarice, sometimes gambled their very souls for this hidden wealth.

One of those who searched and suffered was Abdul Rehman Abu Sultan. He lived in poverty on the edge of the city of Basra, unreconciled to his present life of hardship. His family's lands, close by a river and easily irrigated, had once been fertile, with shoots of green alfalfa and tawny barley springing up effortlessly. Season by season, as the water flooded the lands and the desert heat baked them dry, a film of salt had crept across the soil, bringing ruin to the family.

Abdul passed the winter days bemoaning his lot in the coffee house, where watery sunlight streamed through the mats that covered the walls, lighting up the smoke haze in the air from the charcoal brazier. There, the men of the district huddled together, drinking endless cups of thick, sweet coffee, discussing their troubles. Abdul's voice was always loudest.

One day a stranger happened into their midst. Overhearing their words, he ostentatiously clicked his beads so that the gleaming lapis lazuli shimmered to advantage in the dusty light. Then, with one beringed hand, he adjusted a robe trimmed with gold braid, revealing a precious amulet of silver and turquoise.

Immediately, Abdul's eye was drawn to the gems and gleaming metals. As Abdul held forth to his companions on the unfairness of the world, he covertly observed the stranger and wondered what a person of his wealth was doing in a humble coffee house in this flyblown suburb of the city.

Midday came and, with it, a hunger that Abdul had no money to satisfy. Even the coarsest foods were beyond the reach of his pocket. With ill-concealed envy, he watched the stranger call for a snack of liver and onion broiled over the charcoal fire. The smells of the dish made Abdul's stomach tighten with hunger. The man paid with coins from a bulging purse, ate his fill and left the rest.

With an air of camaraderie, the stranger beckoned to Abdul and his friends, offered them the leftovers from his plate and asked if they would like to hear the story of his life. His audience urged him on. He had been born a poor man, he said, but through determination and a love of adventure he had become a rich merchant and now enjoyed a life of ease. His travels, so he told them, had taken him to many strange and exotic places and had shown him unforgettable sights.

Yet, he said, he still longed for the simple life of his boyhood, and so came to places like this coffee house, where he could talk to men of his own kind.

Flattered, and eager to prove himself as a worthy companion to the stranger, Abdul spoke out against the humble existence that inspired such nostalgia. He painted a grim picture of its miseries and privations, and vowed that he himself would be prepared to do anything to change his lot and become one of the lucky ones who ruled the world and controlled their own destinies.

With a satisfied smile, the stranger told Abdul that he had known him for a brave man from the first moment he had seen him. He assured Abdul that he knew a sure way for such a person to change his fate for the better.

Fascinated, Abdul asked to hear more, and the merchant spoke of a cave in the middle of the desert that was rumored to hold the key to all the wealth and all the wisdom of the world. It was said by the nomads that the way down to the cave was as lonely and terrifying as a journey into one's own grave, and its treasure was guarded by an ancient Queen of the jinn who fed on human souls.

Abdul and his friends were frightened by these words. With a wave of his hand that dismissed the others, the man leaned closer to Abdul and assured him that such talk of graves and jinn was mere superstition. What counted was the treasure itself—jewels so large and brilliant they made a Sultan's gems look like fragments of glass; golden coins thick on the floor; intricately crafted ornaments of the most precious metals, piled high against the walls. All these things were there just for the taking, if one were bold enough and brave enough.

Abdul, his heart ablaze with greed, begged his new acquaintance to reveal the location of the cave. When the merchant promised to take him there, Abdul's friends warned him not to go. It was one thing to dream of riches, they said, but another to steal them from the jinn. Only magic of the blackest sort could have stored up such a treasure as the stranger described, and contact with it would surely stain his soul.

Drawing Abdul aside, his companions questioned the stranger's motives, wondering why he was prepared to let Abdul take the treasure instead of claiming it himself. Perhaps he meant to let Abdul run the risks, and then murder him once he had procured the riches.

Abdul silenced them all with a reproof, reminding them that although the merchant was not one of their own people, they had eaten with him. According to tradition, those who shared meat and salt could trust one another.

The newcomer held his peace as the friends continued to argue, letting the clink of his precious beads and the winking of the stones in his rings remind Abdul of everything that he offered. Finally, Abdul refused to listen to any more warnings and vowed to set off into the desert to find his destiny.

Giving Abdul no time to reconsider his decision, the merchant hired camels, and the two men set out together through the date palm groves along the banks of the River Euphrates. They traveled alone, safe from the prying eyes of bearers and attendants who might steal the treasure. The stranger assured Abdul that his amulet was a powerful one and that neither the jinn nor the tribes of the desert would trouble them.

Then the wasteland lay before them, vast and featureless. Abdul was wary for signs of the evil ones. He looked for men who cast no shadows, cats appearing out of thin air, columns of sand traveling across the horizon, yet he found none of these things.

But there were other, subtler ways of reckoning, and Abdul examined those as well. In the desert's swirling sands, in the mists that rose eerily from the top of their tent in the morning, in the bounding of gazelles, he read disaster. A hawk flew by with its left side to him, and Abdul's skin crawled with a presentiment of doom. They passed a place straight out of hell, where pools of black bitumen bubbled malevolently. And at night when they camped, Abdul dreamed of flames in strange colors. The auguries were all against him. But just as he had finally decided to turn back and go home, a pauper still, to face the jeers of his friends, the stranger pointed out a rise in the sand and announced that at last they had reached their destination.

At the crest of the hill stood an archway of fallen stones, so massive that they could only have been brought to this place by the jinn. Abdul mumbled some holy words to counteract any evil that

In the belly of a cave beneath the desert floor, the treasure-seeker Abdul
encountered a door inscribed with a promise of untold wealth and wisdom.

might linger. Between the great stones lay a narrow opening.

Abdul slowly approached the crevice and peered down into the darkness he was soon to enter. The top steps had been silted over by sand; beneath them lay a void from which came the dank breath of evil. As Abdul again spoke the holy words, the winds of the desert swept the chill away. Looking back at the stranger, Abdul saw him cast down his eyes and finger his beads once more. Then, before Abdul could speak to him, the man and the two camels suddenly vanished. A cloud of dust was the only sign that they had ever been there at all.

Alone beneath the burning sun, Abdul had no choice but to go forward to meet his fate. As he descended the winding stairway that led down to the treasure, he recalled all the tales he had heard of jinn who lurked within the earth—creatures full of baleful cunning, huge enough to tear a man to pieces and evil enough to cause the deaths of whole villages. Step by fearful step, Abdul made his way downward. Blackness enveloped him. At last, at the bottom of the stairway, his hand touched the cold metal of a door.

A sickly luminescence from some unknown source revealed an inscription incised into the brass: "Let the seeker kiss this door if he wishes to enter. He will receive more treasure than he can count and more knowledge than he can speak of." Abdul touched his lips to the ice-cold metal. At once, the door swung open to reveal an inner chamber flooded with unearthly, greenish light.

At first he saw only the treasure piled against the walls—gold and silver coins, embossed trays, filigreed beakers, bejeweled pitchers, sparkling gems, lustrous pearls. He began to fill his pockets with the coins. Then the smell of death that filled the cavern warned him that more than treasure was here.

Around the walls hung the corpses of men. In the breeze from the corridor, their rotting bodies swayed. Some had been reduced to skeletons; their bones clicked against one another. Abdul took a step back, only to be drawn forward again by a voice of irresistible power, commanding him to approach.

At the far end of the cavern, sitting on a pile of precious stones, was a woman more beautiful than any he had ever seen before. She beckoned to him in the wavering light, her shiny black hair falling over her shoulders, her red lips eager, her dark eyes compelling. Abdul inched forward, entranced by her beauty, forgetting that only a daughter of night, a female jinni, would dwell under the earth guarding a mountain of treasure.

She bade him come closer. Then she promised that all the riches of the world would be his, and all the wisdom of the world as well, if only he would take her in his arms and kiss her. The shining limbs of the woman stretched forward, drawing Abdul to her, making him forget the stench of death that filled his nostrils and the silent strangers lining the walls.

The woman's flesh was clammy, and her hair reeked of the charnel house, but Abdul clasped her firmly to him. All

Within the chamber Abdul spied a naked woman seated upon a heap of coins and jewels. Attending her was a silent court of skeletons, dangling from the cavern walls.

around him jewels winked and gold glistened; emeralds and rubies and diamonds shifted beneath his feet. Abdul pressed his lips to hers.

The woman clasped him with super-human force, drawing his tongue into her mouth until flesh could stretch no farther. Then, with a surge of unearthly power, she pulled Abdul's tongue out by its roots, leaving a bloody, gaping hole where it had been. Into that gulf came the woman's tongue, implanting itself in the warm, sticky wound and stopping the gushing blood that spurted forth.

As Abdul drew away, the woman fell, lifeless, from his arms, the flesh draining from her body into a putrefying slime. It fell in puddles over the winking gems, clouding their brilliance. Abdul stepped back from the whitened bones that protruded from the green and viscous mass. Heedless now of the fortune at hand, he ran from the terrible place.

An alien voice issued from his own mouth and stopped Abdul's flight. The voice announced that from now on Abdul would do its bidding. So long as Abdul followed the tongue's instructions, he would receive all the wealth he desired, but any disobedience would be harshly punished. Abdul opened his mouth to say a prayer that would banish this evil. His throat worked convulsively, but no words came out. He tried to scream, but could not. At last his mouth produced a sound—the high-pitched laughter of the tongue.

Abdul stumbled out of the cave and began to walk across the burning sands. The clinking of the coins he had stuffed into his pockets in those first blissful moments in the cave mocked his every step. From time to time the tongue issued commands, making him turn first to the right, then to the left. He obeyed, imagining the horrors that would befall him if he did not. After a while an oasis appeared in the distance. The tongue instructed Abdul to walk toward it.

By the side of a well at the center of the oasis stood a clay jar. Abdul filled it up with water. With trembling hands, he raised the jug to his parched lips and drank, but he could taste nothing. Despairing, he dropped the vessel. The tongue ordered him to move on.

Near Basra the land grew green again. Groves of eucalyptus, orange and lemon trees scented the air, and the fronds of date palms waved overhead. The tongue directed Abdul through the busy streets into the souk, taking him past shops containing the wealth of the world: silks from the East, their colors brilliant under the Arabian sun; rare and costly spices that promised delights to the palate; songbirds whose tongues trilled melodies to enchant the ear; carpets woven in intricate patterns, each thread saturated with rich dyes. All these things he coveted, but most of all he wanted food. Delicious aromas drew him to an expensive eating house. The tongue instructed him to enter, and ordered a dinner fit for a King. Here were dishes Abdul had only dreamed of: stuffed nightingale marinated in crimson pomegranate juice, the finest rice pilaff cooked with almonds, raisins and golden saffron; tender eggplants infused with coriander and cloves; coffee flavored with ground amber.

Abdul took up one delicacy after another, chewing each and finding it as devoid of savor as the stale barley bread he had eaten while a pauper. After a time, he was maddened by the odor of spices and rosewater, roast fowl and sweet cinnamon, for he could taste none of the delights they promised. The tongue praised each dish as it appeared, describing the flavors in rapturous terms as Abdul filled his hungry belly with food that gave no pleasure. Then, surfeited at last, the tongue ordered Abdul out of the souk and into the familiar alleyways that led to his own district of the city.

Nothing had changed in the coffee house. His friends sat, as they always had, idling the day away with gossip. When they saw Abdul, they asked if he had found the treasure. Laughing, they pointed at his torn and dirty clothes, assuming that his trip to the desert had amounted to nothing.

The tongue answered for him, telling them to cease their mockery, but the jeers only grew louder. Then the tongue hailed two of the men by name. It invited Ibrahim to look at Ali's arm, and pointed out the streaks of bright red plaster dust that stained it.

Wasn't it Ibrahim, asked the tongue, who had but yesterday plastered the wall behind his own marriage bed? Ibrahim looked startled, but nodded. And how odd it was, continued the tongue, that his friend Ali bore marks that could only have been acquired if he had slept that very morning with Ibrahim's wife.

Enraged, the cuckolded husband pulled out a knife from his belt and raised it against Ali, to avenge his honor. Ali drew his own blade in turn, and the two men lunged fiercely at one other. An instant later, both lay dead, their blood pooling on the floor of the coffee shop. The onlookers turned accusing eyes on Abdul, whose words had caused this murderous rupture of a friendship.

Fearing that the tongue would do even more damage, Abdul ran toward his hut. His wife saw him coming and emerged to greet him. He held out his arms to her, sure of a haven at last. But the tongue began to call all the neighbors together. Once the occupants of the nearby huts had assembled, the women wiping their hands on aprons, the men abandoning their water pipes, the tongue uttered the well-known formula that allowed a husband to rid himself of his mate: "I divorce thee. I divorce thee. I divorce thee." Abdul watched helplessly as his wife backed away, howling with anguish. In accordance with ancient custom, the tongue pronounced the declaration of divorcement three times, making the act final.

The neighbors shook their heads at Abdul's behavior. Some whispered that his wife was lucky to be rid of him, for he seemed to have gone quite mad. His lips had spoken the decree gladly, but his eyes and face had shown only horror and sorrow.

Inside the hut, Abdul's son lay crying. His father's strange behavior and his mother's tears had terrified him. Abdul

Enslaved by a force he could not exorcise, Abdul heard his tongue
utter words against his will. They drove his wife away forever,
tricked his friends into murder and lured his son to sudden death.

went toward his beloved boy, his first and only child, who would soon be old enough to recite the Koran. Before he could reach out to comfort him, however, he heard the tongue order the child up from his mat and out of the house.

His father followed, filled with a terrible sense of foreboding. The tongue commanded the child to run to a nearby well that had long since run dry and stand on the wall surrounding it. Seeing his son balanced so precariously, Abdul hastened to him, but as he ran, the tongue gave a bloodcurdling scream. The child started, lost his balance and plunged down the shaft, snapping his neck at the bottom.

Abdul rushed to the wall and looked into the pit where the body of his son sprawled like a broken doll at the bottom. His heart lifted for a moment when he thought he perceived a faint stirring of the boy's limbs. But he soon realized that what he saw was simply a pair of lizards, scuttling over the corpse that had arrived so suddenly in their domain.

Unshed tears burned in Abdul's eyes, and his face contorted in a rictus of agony. He choked with the effort to wail his misery, but no sound came from his parted lips.

The tongue forced Abdul to move on. As he walked away from the well, his wife's wild ululations of grief followed him. He tore at his hair and rent his clothes, spilling the coins in his pockets, heedless now of their value.

From then on, Abdul thought only of ridding himself of the loathsome object that had taken root in his mouth and ruined his life. Again and again he direc-ted his steps toward the sacred places of the city, knowing that there his curse could be exorcised, for evil could not withstand the holy words. But each time that he drew near to a mosque or a shrine, the tongue curled back in his throat, choking him, until he was forced to turn away or die.

One night, near the market stalls of the food vendors on the banks of the Euphrates, the tongue supped on the tender flesh of grilled fish. While chewing the morsels he could not taste, Abdul saw a holy man walking by the riverside, bending low over his prayer beads as he recited his devotions. Before the tongue could stop him, Abdul leaped up and wrote a message in the sand. It begged the saintly dervish to say the prayer for banishing evil spirits. The man observed Abdul's stricken face, then swiftly complied. When he recited the holy lines, the tongue began to shudder and shiver within Abdul's mouth, knocking him off balance and throwing him backward into the dark waters of the river.

The tongue flew out of his mouth and disappeared, like a fat black eel, in the muddy current. Abdul, treading water, saw four huge fish, their fins glistening in the moonlight, heading toward him. Abdul, tongueless, could not scream as the great jagged jaws battered onto him. The creatures savaged at Abdul's limbs, until the holy man saw the blood billowing in the water and dived in to rescue him. Not daring to harm the dervish, the fish swam away. The man dragged Abdul out of the

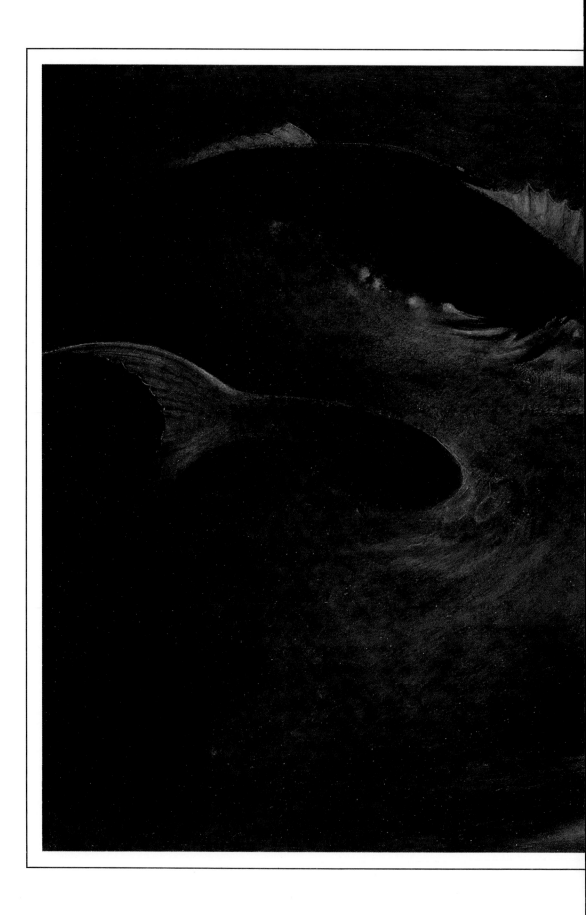

Four great fishes, razor-jawed, advanced on Abdul when he fell into the river.

Before his rescuers could reach him, all his limbs were snapped off and devoured.

water and summoned help from the net-menders working nearby. When they placed him gently on the riverbank, near the fire of an itinerant fish-seller, they could see that Abdul's arms and legs had been bitten off.

Abdul was carried to a doctor, who cauterized the blood vessels and bound up the stumps. Puzzled when his patient did not emit the usual screams, the physician saw that Abdul had no tongue. It soon became clear that Abdul's reason had left him as well. His gaze was dull and vacant. His mouth moved in endless insane mumblings, but without a tongue he could not make a sound.

As Abdul's wounds healed, and his fever subsided, he was fed on gruel by the doctor's servants. Finally, the physician pronounced him as strong and fit as he could ever hope to be. No kinfolk came to claim him, and no friends appeared to care for him, so he was taken to the market to live as a beggar. Day after day, in all weathers and seasons, he sat against a wall in the great souk of Basra, as all the treasures of the world were paraded past his uncaring eyes. No longer did he ache to possess the fine porcelains of China, the spices of India, the ivory and gold dust of Africa, or the silk of Turkestan.

Passersby stuffed morsels of bread or dried dates into his mouth, for it was a blessing to feed a beggar. Those who were too poor to spare a mouthful of food filled their own begging cups with water and tipped it into his slack mouth, drop by drop. The wealthy scattered coins and jewels at his feet. But Abdul no longer knew or cared what money was, and had forgotten how to spend it. Some merchants, travelers from the east, left him pieces of lapis lazuli that winked as seductively as the stranger's blue prayer beads in the coffee shop so long ago. But Abdul was now immune to the lure of cold stone. If any memories piqued or plagued him, he had no means to share them.

As time passed, he became known throughout the city, until finally even the Caliph in his palace had heard of him. He asked to be told the story of Abdul's life, and of how he had come, mute and limbless, to take his place as a beggar in the marketplace, the most conspicuous among Basra's vast and miserable tribe of mendicants.

The Caliph sent his agents to make inquiries in the myriad alleyways and narrow passages of all the souks and suburbs. From Abdul's friends in the coffee house they learned of the mysterious stranger who had tempted the poor man with his tale of boundless riches, and of his cryptic promise of infinite wealth and wisdom. The Caliph ordered a plaque to be placed over Abdul's head as a warning to others who might be tempted by poverty to seek the treasures of the jinn.

The brass legend explained the plight of the speechless and empty-eyed human wreck who sat beneath it through all the hot and airless days of summer and the numbing winter rains. Here was a man, it said, to whom the jinn had promised, and had given, more knowledge than he could speak of and more riches than he could count.

•12•

Demons of the Dreamtime

The tribes of Australia knew the season for every fruit, the call of every bird, the depth of every water hole. But they also knew that their land held terrible secrets and harbored creatures that hated humankind.

One of these beings was Garkain, the jealous guardian of the steaming mangrove forest that fringed Australia's northern shore. All the tribes of the region feared him, though few had seen his form. But it was known that he dwelled alone, without mate or young, and cherished his solitude.

The size of a man, Garkain had batlike wings that carried him heavily from branch to branch. Should any lost child or rash hunter enter his territory, he swooped. The rustling wings would shroud the victim, who choked from the stench of that alien flesh, struggled feebly, and then slowly suffocated. Once his quarry lay still, Garkain tore the body limb from limb and wolfed the raw flesh. And forevermore the spirit of the intruder was condemned to walk in anguish, lost among the great trees and grasses of that region, unable to find its way home to the ancient resting-place of its tribe.

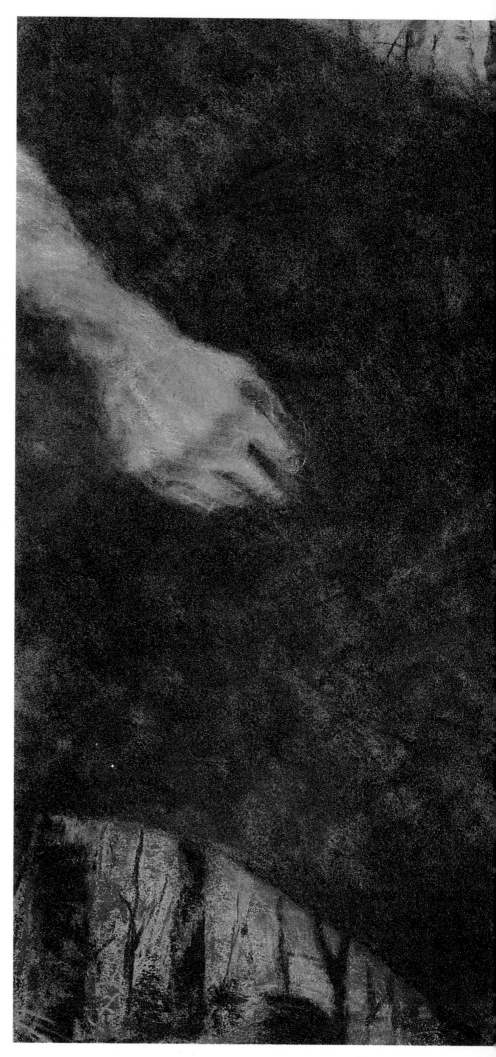

The Myndie Snake

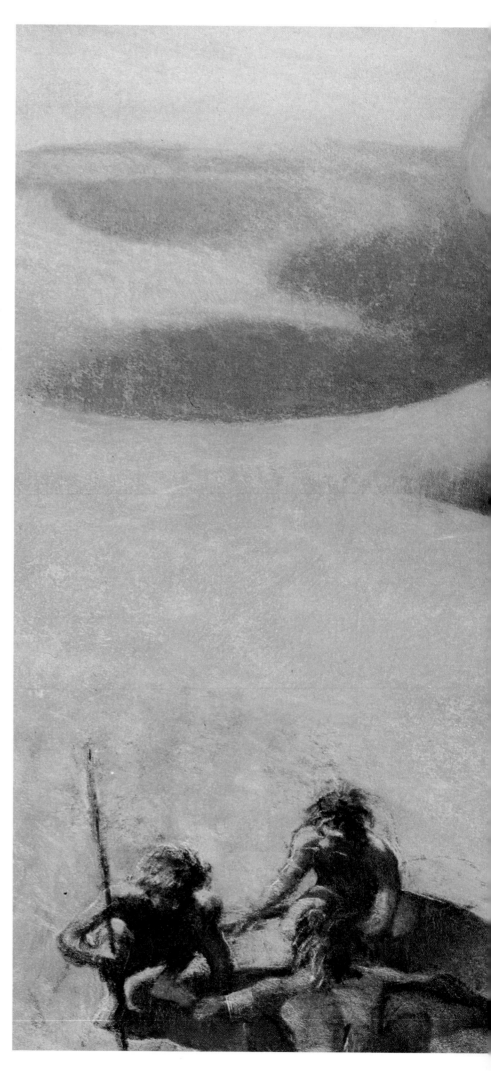

Beings stranger even than Garkain wrought evil in Australia's outback—the empty hinterland where the sun beat down on rust-red sand, shimmering saltpans and ancient, eroded hills. Dazzled by the searing light, those people who walked the wilderness knew never to trust the images before their eyes.

In the evening, when men, women and children gathered around their camp fires, the hills sometimes seemed to draw closer. Then storytellers warned of a serpent ten miles long that slid across the land like a moving mountain range. This was the Myndie snake, the terrible instrument of Pundjil, creator of all the universe.

Transgressors of Pundjil's laws listened in dread for the sibilant voice of his servant. When they heard a hissing on the wind, they knew their crimes had caught up with them. They dropped their spears and shields, abandoned their dogs and their children, and ran for cover into the bush. But there was no escape. Those who had sinned, violated taboos, or otherwise incurred their creator's wrath were easily flushed out. The avenging serpent could see and hear for many miles in all directions and moved with a speed that belied its massive size.

Its victims' fate was always the same. Crouched in their hiding-holes, they felt drops of a burning rain and looked up to see cavernous jaws dripping venom. But they saw nothing else, for the Myndie's bite was swift. Heavy-bellied, the serpent would slide away to wait again for Pundjil's summons.

The Devil-Dog

When hot winds howled across the outback, a terrible transformation sometimes took place amid the swirling sand. Somewhere out of sight, a creature that wore the shape of a man lay down and let the drifting sand blanket him. There he slept until the storm abated. When the shriek of the butcher bird pierced the air, the crust of the dune that hid him trembled and broke. Sand streamed from a bristled muzzle, a lolling tongue, a fanged jaw. Irrinja, the devil-dog, big as the dune itself, rose, hungry for flesh.

Tale-spinners spoke of a certain hunting party that left one of their number to continue the chase when they made camp for the night. As the lone hunter tracked his quarry, he could hear his comrades' songs. Then an unnatural silence fell. Alarmed, he sped to the camp and found nothing but a great pool of blood.

He felt a scorching breath on his shoulder and found himself staring up into the red eyes of the giant devil-dog. Irrinja leaped, but the hunter slashed with his knife. The blade sliced through fur and flesh from ear to ear. The creature's victims tumbled out, still alive, from his torn throat.

At that, Irrinja fled into the darkness, running first on four legs, then on two. Shrinking with each step he took, he shed his canine hide, his incisors and blood-encrusted claws. Man-shaped once more, he stumbled across the dunes until he fell. In time, blowing sand would cover him over and he would sleep, waiting for the cry of the butcher bird.

The Whowie

The tribes of Australia's riverlands told of a season when their ancestors were plagued by an unknown destroyer. Young men went on walkabout and never returned; mothers woke to find their children snatched from their sides; men standing sentry were seized if their weary eyes closed for an instant.

After many such losses, a search party, scouring the banks of a nearby river, came upon blood-soaked rocks and churned sandbanks. Then they sighted their enemy, sunning itself on an outcrop. Shaped like a lizard, twenty feet long, it supported its great weight on six legs. Its face was hideous, its mouth capacious enough to swallow a man at one gulp. The terrified witnesses fled.

The monster, which the tribesmen named the Whowie, always struck while its victims slept. One night it lumbered toward a camp fire and devoured everyone around it, sixty souls in all. Summoning up their courage, hunters from all the neighboring encampments traced the beast's clawprints to a cave in the riverbank. Knowing that the Whowie would be sluggish after gorging, they stacked green wood at the mouth of the cave and made a fire to smoke the reptile out. Soon the earth juddered as the Whowie coughed and lurched toward fresh air.

When the great beast staggered from the cave opening, the hunters plunged their spears into its sides and battered its head with clubs. Roars filled the valley, and then faded away to a gurgling groan. At last, the Whowie was no more. But many years of rain and wind were needed to wear away the blood that stained its trail.

·13·

The Healer's Secret

There was ample work for Death to do on the bleached hillsides and arid plateaus of old Spain. Plague, brigands, hunger, and the hot quarrels of marketplace and marriage bed took their bloody toll. The justice of Kings and priests was unforgiving. Thieves and heretics had no second chances: They learned their lessons with grim finality, strangled by a twist of the garrote, or roasted alive by hooded executioners.

In those days, said the storytellers, Death walked the world in human shape, sometimes in the form of a woman. Those travelers who chanced to meet her on the road would stand aside and pray silently that she would pass them by. Yet a tale was told of a time when she did not pass, but paused to strike a bargain.

The other party to the transaction was a poor rustic, slightly tipsy from a night of celebration: His wife had just presented him with a son. Flown with wine and fatherhood, he wandered through the mountains near his home, pondering how best to give the boy a good start in life.

The only way a person of low degree could rise in the world was through the help of a powerful patron. The man resolved to find a godparent who, linked by spiritual ties as strong as those of blood, would provide support and protection.

As the peasant negotiated a narrow mountain path, an enormous, shrouded figure blocked his passage. He recognized the pale gleam of a grinning skull within the shadow of the hood. It was Death. With his heart in his throat, he asked if she had come to claim his life. She replied that his hour had not yet arrived, but that she wished to offer herself as godmother to his child.

Something in her tone soothed his terrors. The peasant pondered. He realized the strange proposal had much to recommend it. Death was indeed the most powerful figure known to humankind. She was universally feared and respected; no one could escape the finality of her decisions, nor the incorruptible impartiality of her judgments. Looking her in the eye, he welcomed the suggestion and bade her come to the christening, fixed for the following week. Death offered no felicitations, but stated flatly that the man would not regret his decision. She

When a Spanish peasant vowed to find his son
a powerful godparent, Death herself
volunteered to hold the infant at the font.

promised that her godson would achieve wealth and position. Then she vanished.

With Death's hollow tones ringing in his ears, the peasant hurried home to tell his news. Until the day of the christening, the neighbors spoke of nothing else. And, try as he might, the priest who was to carry out the baptism could find no way of avoiding his duties.

Death's gaunt figure appeared in the church at the stroke of the appointed hour, and moved with stately tread through the stunned and silent congregation. When the child had been christened, Death handed the father a heavy pouch of gold and told him that she would return when the boy was twenty. As the assembled villagers watched with fascinated dread, she stretched out her skeletal hand, lightly touched the baby's forehead and glided away.

The child grew up to be strong and healthy. Death's gift of gold ensured that the family never lacked for anything. But they looked forward with trepidation to her promised return.

When the boy's twentieth birthday came, his family marked it with a feast. Precisely at midday, a cold gust blew open the door and Death stood before them. She wished her godson happiness and, as a godmother should, expressed pleasure at seeing him grown so strong and handsome. Then she led him into another room, her bony fingertips resting lightly but possessively on his sleeve.

When they were alone, Death took out from the recesses of her shroud an earthenware pot. It contained a plant unlike any he had seen before. It had leaves the color of a bruise and tiny white flowers that almost looked like skulls and gave off a faint but pervasive odor he could not identify. She explained that it was an herb of supernatural power. It would make him the most successful and respected physician in all of Spain.

Whenever he visited a sick person, she said, he was to glance immediately at the ends of the bed. If he saw Death standing at the head of the patient, he should provide a sprig of the herb to be brewed up into an infusion. When the sick person drank this, he would recover. But if the doctor saw Death's figure standing at the foot, it meant the patient was doomed. He was on no account to use the magic herb to flout destiny.

The godmother assured the youth that the plant would stay fresh and green forever and that no eyes but his own would be able to discern her presence. Then she pressed his shoulder lightly with the cold points of her fingers, and slipped away.

In time, everything Death promised came to pass. The youth first cured an ailing neighbor, then a priest, then a wealthy merchant, next a lawyer, and finally a duke. Stories of his success spread further and further afield until the whole of Spain knew of his fame. No one could tell where he had studied or who his professors had been; he never quoted Hippocrates or Galen in the original Greek or Latin; he employed none of the other herbal remedies that were in common use; but no one doubted his superiority even to the best-qualified and most senior

As a gift to her godchild, Death offered an herb that would heal the sick, howeve
grave their maladies. But she gave strict instructions for its
use, and warned the youth that it would go ill with him to flout them.

graybeards, for when he dosed a sufferer, the patient always healed in three days.

More sinister but equally impressive was the fact that if he declined to treat a patient, then without exception the victim died soon afterward. To watch the famous young physician turn sorrowfully away from a sickbed was to feel the chill breath of the grave. With such testimonials, the young man soon became the most sought-after doctor in the kingdom. His fees were as high as he chose to set them, and his peasant origins were left far behind, for he came to be accepted as a scholar, a gentleman and an equal in all the great houses of Spain.

The day came when the doctor was summoned to the bedside of the King himself. The monarch was failing. He had been a just and merciful ruler, and his loss would be sincerely mourned; but worse, since he had no son, his successor would be a cruel, corrupt nephew whose rule was certain to bring nothing but evil.

Arriving at the palace, the doctor was greeted by the King's daughter, who begged him to do everything possible to save her father's life. The young physician was not immune to the Princess's beauty, nor to the trusting candor of her gaze. Devoutly hoping that he would find Godmother Death in the place that meant life, he hastened into the royal apartments. On the ornate bed lay the emaciated body of the King, as still as an effigy on a tomb. Empty shadows shrouded the head of the bed; at the foot was the dark, veiled form of Death.

Unable to control his disappointment, the doctor spent several minutes pretend-ing to examine the King. He opened his mouth to explain that it was not possible to save the King's life. But he found himself swallowing the words and promising instead that the patient would recover. He then administered the healing herb.

Fear made him put off going home until late in the day. As dusk was gathering, he returned with dragging steps to a house that was as dank as the grave. He walked, footsteps echoing, from one empty room to the next, until he reached his study. There, in her shroud, stood Death, incandescent with anger. The physician pleaded that he had disobeyed her in spite of himself; his pity for the Princess and his anxiety for the country's welfare had prevailed over his better judgment. After a pause, Death said that she would pardon him once and once only. She knew that he had not acted out of selfish ambition. But if he disobeyed her again, she would show no mercy. The doctor kept his own counsel about the events of that night, and if he thought of Death's warning he gave no sign.

The next two years were happy ones. He was appointed personal physician to the King and became one of his most trusted advisers. His wealth and power outstripped all the court grandees, but his greatest joy was his love for the Princess. The King made it plain that, in spite of the doctor's humble birth, the couple would be permitted to marry.

Then, without warning, a shadow fell across their happiness. The Princess became ill in the night. The next day,

Furious at his disobedience, Death warned the godson that he would not be given a second chance to countermand her wishes.

Though he had risen to be the greatest physician in the
 land, the young man learned that his powers were useless
 when his godmother saw fit to claim his royal fiancée.

when her fiancé came, as was his custom, to pay his respects, he was told of her condition. A maidservant said that she had taken to her bed shortly after supper, complaining of chills and fever. But she had refused to permit her attendants to summon the doctor from his home. She insisted that her beloved be allowed to rest from his daily labors undisturbed, and she would not countenance her own petty complaints being the cause of any inconvenience to him. As the night drew on, however, the Princess's condition had rapidly grown worse.

The physician pushed past the maidservant and entered the bedchamber. He lifted his eyes, with dread in his heart, to the foot of the Princess's bed. There—it was as if he had known it already—he saw Death gazing blankly toward him. He did not glance in her direction again, but busied himself with comforting and tending his fiancée. Bending close to the Princess's burning cheek, the doctor murmured that she was to fear nothing, for he would make her well again. In spite of her pain, the Princess smiled, trusting completely in his skill.

He recalled his godmother's warning, but pushed her threats from his mind. The only thing that mattered was the rescue of his beloved. He hurried home to fetch the herb. But Death was there before him, waiting in the study. She stood in front of the hearth, tearing up the leaves of the plant she had given him and tossing the fragments into the fire. The pot that had held the herb lay broken at her feet. She expressed no anger; the time for that was past. Instead, she commanded him to follow her. She had something to show him.

Without knowing how, he traveled with his godmother as she passed soundlessly over mountains, plains and broad rivers, until they came to a barren valley littered with chalk-white boulders and naked stones. Death paused at the dark mouth of a gigantic cavern, and beckoned the young man to follow her inside. The floor of the great cave stretched away as far as the eye could see, covered with countless thousands of lighted candles—some tall, some short.

Death explained that every candle represented a human life: The tallest were those of newborn children who had the longest to live, the medium-sized ones were those of people who had reached their prime of life, and those with only a short length left to burn belonged to the old or to the mortally ill.

As she passed between the candles, Death stopped in front of a guttering flame that seemed on the point of going out. Sick at heart, the doctor asked whose it was. His godmother told him what he had already guessed: that it was the candle of his beloved Princess, whose end no force could prevent. Another, stronger taper burned brightly at its side.

"Yours," said Death. "You say you cannot live without her. Very well. Then take this as a gift, and not a punishment."

With a single, icy breath, she blew both candles out. The doctor fell in a lifeless heap at her feet. And, far away in the capital, a church bell began to toll.

In a cavern in the wilderness, burning candles marked the
length of human lives. When Death decreed
it, the lights of the two lovers guttered and went out.

Acknowledgments

The editors wish to thank the following for their assistance in the preparation of this volume: Tony Allan, London; Guy Andrews, London; Lesley Coleman, London; Fergus Fleming, London; John Gaisford, London; Avril Hart, Victoria and Albert Museum, London; Ann House, Canada House, London; Elizabeth Ketchum, Canada House, London; Jackie Matthews, London; Ann Natanson, Rome; Venetia Newell, London; Aagot Noss, Norsk Folkemuseum, Oslo; Robin Olson, London; Paul Smith, Doncaster, England; Naomi Tarrant, Royal Scottish Museum, Edinburgh; Deborah Thompson, London; Linda Wooley, Victoria and Albert Museum, London.

Picture Credits

The sources for the illustrations in this book are shown below.

Cover: Artwork by Matt Mahurin. 1-5: Artwork by Graham Ward. 6-21: Artwork by Mark Langeneckert. 23-27: Artwork by John Sibbick. 28-35: Artwork by Graham Ward. 36-53: Artwork by Gary Kelley. 55-60: Artwork by Matt Mahurin. 62-69: Artwork by Nick Harris. 71-77: Artwork by Stuart Robertson. 78-86: Artwork by Matt Mahurin. 89-95: Artwork by George Tute. 97-105: Artwork by John Howe. 106-121: Artwork by Susan Gallagher. 122-129: Artwork by Mark Langeneckert. 131-139: Artwork by Kevin Grey. 144: Artwork by Graham Ward.

Bibliography

Aldington, Richard, and Delano Ames, transl., *New Larousse Encyclopedia of Mythology.* London: The Hamlyn Publishing Group, 1985.*

Alexander, Hartley Burr, *The Mythology of All Races: North American.* Vol. 10. New York: Cooper Square Publications, 1964.

Allen, Louis A, *Time Before Morning.* New York: Thomas Y. Crowell Company, 1975.*

The Australian Encyclopaedia. Vol. 1. Sydney: The Grolier Society of Australia, 1983.

Bain, R. Nisbet, *Weird Tales from Northern Seas from the Danish of Jonas Lie.* London: Kegan Paul, Trench, Trubner, 1893.*

Bancroft-Hunter, Norman, *People of the Totem.* London: Orbis Publishing, 1979.*

Balikci, Asen, "Female Infanticide on the Arctic Coast." *Man,* December 1967.

Baring-Gould, S., *Curious Myths of The Middle Ages.* London: Longmans, Green, 1897.*

Barrett, Charles, *The Bunyip.* Melbourne: Reed & Harris, 1946.

Bassett, Fletcher S., *Legends and Superstitions of the Sea and of Sailors.* London: Sampson Low, Marston, Searle & Rivington, 1885.

Ben-Amos, Dan:
In Praise of The Baal Shem Tov (Shivhei La-Besht). Transl. and ed. by Jerome R. Mintz. Bloomington: Indiana University Press, no date.
The Earliest Collection of Legends about the Founder of Hasidism. Bloomington/London: Indiana University Press, no date.

Berndt, Ronald M., *Australian Aboriginal Religion.* Leiden: E. J. Brill, 1974.*

Berndt, Ronald M., and Catherine H. Berndt, *The World of the First Australians.* London: Angus and Robertson, 1964.

Boas, Franz, *Kwakiuti Culture as Reflected in Mythology.* New York: American Folk-Lore Society, 1935.

Bonnard, André, *Greek Civilization.* Transl. by A. Lytton Sells. London: George Allen & Unwin, 1962.

Bozic, Sreten, *Aboriginal Myths.* Melbourne: Gold Star Publications, 1972.

Briggs, Jean, *Never in Anger.* Cambridge: Harvard University Press, 1970.*

Bringsvaerd, Tor Age, *Phantoms and Fairies from Norwegian Folklore.* Transl. by Pat Paw. Oslo: Tahum-Norli, 1979.

Castiglioni, Arturo, M.D., *A History of Medicine.* Transl. and ed. by E.B. Krumbhaar, M.D., Ph.D. New York: Alfred A. Knopf, 1947.

Cavendish, Richard, *Man, Myth and Magic.* New York: Marshall

Cavendish, 1970.*

Cole, Joanna, *Best Loved Folktales*. New York: Doubleday, 1982.*

Comyns, Mrs. Carr, *Northern Italian Folk*. London: Chatto and Windus, 1878.

Craigie, W.A.:
The Icelandic Sagas. Cambridge: Cambridge University Press, 1913.*
Scandinavian Folklore. London: Alexander Gardner, 1896.*
Myths of Northern Europe. Harmondsworth, England: Penguin Books, 1964.

Davidson, Hilda R. Ellis, and W.M.S. Russell, *The Folklore of Ghosts*. Cambridge: D.S. Brewer, 1980-81.*

Davis, Wade, *The Serpent and the Rainbow*. London: Collins, 1986.

Dixon, Roland B., *The Mythology of All Races: Oceanic*. Vol. 9. Boston: Marshall Jones Company, 1916.

Elaide, Mircea, *Australian Religions*. Ithaca: Cornell University Press, 1977.

Faggin, Giorgio, *Fiabe Friulane*. Transl. by Carlo Sgorlon. Milan: Mondadori, 1982.*

Fernea, Elizabeth Warnock, *Guests of the Sheik*. London: Robert Hale, 1968.*

Firth, Alfred, *French Life and Landscape*. London and New York: Paul Elek, 1950.

Foote, P.G., and D.M. Wilson, *The Viking Achievement*. London: Sidgwick & Jackson, 1980.*

Giles, Herbert A., transl., *Strange Stories from a Chinese Studio*. London: T. Werner Laurie, 1916.*

Graves, Robert, *The Greek Myths*. Vols. 1 and 2. Harmondsworth, England: Penguin Books, 1985.

Hart, Martin, *Rats*. Transl. by Arnold Pomerans. London: Alison & Busby, 1982.

Harvey, Sir Paul, *The Oxford Companion to Classical Literature*. Oxford: Oxford University Press,

1984.

Hayter, Colonel F.J., *Deadly Magic*. London: Rider & Co., no date.

Hearn, Lafcadio, *Kwaidan*. London: Kegan Paul, Trench Trubner, 1905.*

Henderson, Ebenezer, *Iceland, or the Journal of Residence in that Land*. London: T. Hamilton, J. Hatchard and L.B. Serley, 1819.

Howells, W.D., *Venetian Life*. Boston: Leighton, Mifflin and Company, The Riverside Press, 1881.

Inverarity, Robert Bruce, *Art of the Northwest Coast Indians*. Berkeley: University of California Press, 1950.

Johnson, W. Branch, *Folktales of Brittany*. London: Methuen and Co. Ltd., 1927.

Joly, Henri L., *Legend in Japanese Art*. London: John Lane The Bodley Head, 1908.*

J.S.F., *Demonologia*. London: A.K. Newman & Co., 1831.

Knowlson, Sharper T., *The Origins of Popular Superstitions and Customs*. London: T. Werner Laurie, 1910.

Lane, Edward, *Arabian Society in The Middle Ages*. Ed. by Stanley Lane-Poole. London: Chatto and Windus, 1883.*

Lang, Andrew, *The Book of Dreams and Ghosts*. New York: Longmans, Green, 1899.*

Leach, Maria, ed., *Funk & Wagnalls Standard Dictionary of Folklore, Mythology and Legend*. San Francisco: Harper & Row, 1984.*

Le Bruz, Anatole, *The Celtic Legend of the Beyond*. Transl. by Derek Bryce. Lampeter, Dyfed, Wales: Llanerch Enterprises, 1986.*

Levin, Meyer, *Classic Hassidic Tales*. New York: The Citadel Press, 1966.*

Lovejoy, Bahija, *The Land and People of Iraq*. Philadelphia: J.B.

Lippincott, 1964.

Lubell, Cecil, ed., *Textile Collections of the World*. Vols. 1 and 2. New York: Van Nostrand Reinhold, 1976.

MacCulloch, J.A.:
The Celtic and Scandinavian Religions. New York: Hutchinson's University Library, 1948.*
The Mythology of All Races: Eddic. Vol. 2. Boston: Marshall Jones Company, 1930.*
Religion of the Ancient Celts. Edinburgh: T. & T. Clark, 1911.*

Magnusson, Magnus, *Hammer of the North*. London: Orbis Publishing, 1976.

Malaurie, Jean, *The Last Kings of Thule*. Transl. by Adrienne Foulke. London: Jonathan Cape, 1982.*

Michener, James A., *Iberia: Spanish Travels and Reflections*. New York: Random House, 1968.

Mountford, Charles P., *Ayers Rock*. Sydney: Angus & Robertson, 1965.

Nangan, Joe, and Hugh Edwards, *Joe Nangan's Dreaming*. Melbourne: Nelson, 1976.*

Palmer, Kingsley, *The Folklore of Somerset*. London: B.T. Batsford Ltd., 1976.

Piggott, Juliet, *Japanese Mythology*. Feltham, England: Newnes Books, 1984.*

Price, David, *The Other Italy*. London: The Olive Press, 1983.

Puckle, Bertram S., *Funeral Customs - The Origin and Development*. London: T. Werner Laurie Ltd., 1926.

Ramsay-Smith, W., *Myths and Legends of The Australian Aboriginals*. London: George C. Harrap, 1930.*

Rasmussen, Knud, *Across Arctic America*. New York: G.P. Putnam's Sons, 1927.

Reed, A.W., *Myths and Legends of Australia*. Sydney: A.H. and A.W. Reed, 1965.

Rink, Henrik, *Tales and Traditions of the Eskimo*. New Introduction by Helge Larsen. Montreal: McGill Queen's University Press, 1974.*

Riordan, James, *A World of Folk-Tales*. London: Hamlyn, 1981.

Roberts, Ainslie, and Charles P. Mountford, *The Dreamtime Book*. Adelaide: Rigby, 1973.*

Schach, Paul, transl., *Eyrbyggja Saga*. Introduction by Lee M. Hollander. Lincoln, Nebraska: University of Nebraska Press, 1959.*

Scott, A.C., *The Kabuki Theatre of Japan*. London: George Allen & Unwin, 1955.

Sebillot, Paul:
Le Folk-Lore de France. Vol. 7. Paris: Librairie Orientale & Américaine, 1904.*
Traditions de la Haute Bretagne.

Vols. 1 and 2. Paris: Maisonneuve, 1882.*

Simpson, Jacqueline, *Icelandic Folktales and Legends*. Berkeley: University of California Press, 1972.

Stevens, E.S., *Folk-Tales of Iraq*. London: Oxford University Press, 1931.*

Taylor, Joseph, *The Danger of Premature Interment*. Printed for W. Simpkin and R. Marshall, 1816.

Treston, Hubert J., *Poine, A Study in Ancient Greek Blood Vengeance*. London: Longmans, Green, 1923.

Turville-Petre, G.:
Myth and Religion of the North. London: Weidenfeld and Nicolson, 1964.
Origins of Icelandic Literature. Oxford: Clarendon Press, 1953.

Vernaut, Jean-Pierre, *Myth and Society in Ancient Greece*. Brighton, Sussex: Harvester Press, 1980.

Walker, Barbara G., *The Women's Encyclopaedia of Myths and Secrets*. San Francisco: Harper & Row, 1983.

Weber, F. Parkes, M.D., *Aspects of Death*. London: T. Fisher Unwin, 1914.

Westermarck, Edward, *Ritual and Belief in Morocco*. London: Macmillan, 1926.*

Young, Gavin, *Iraq: Land of Two Rivers*. London: Collins, 1980.

Zimmels, H.J., Ph.D., *Magicians, Theologians and Doctors*. London: Edward Goldston & Son, 1952.

* *Titles marked with an asterisk were especially helpful in the preparation of this volume.*

Time-Life Books Inc.
is a wholly owned subsidiary of

TIME INCORPORATED

FOUNDER: Henry R. Luce 1898-1967

Editor-in-Chief: Henry Anatole Grunwald
Chairman and Chief Executive Officer: J. Richard
Munro
President and Chief Operating Officer: N. J.
Nicholas Jr.
Chairman of the Executive Committee: Ralph
P. Davidson
Corporate Editor: Ray Cave
Group Vice President, Books: Kelso F. Sutton
Vice President, Books: George Artandi

TIME-LIFE BOOKS INC.

EDITOR: George Constable
Director of Design: Louis Klein
Director of Editorial Resources: Phyllis K. Wise
Acting Text Director: Ellen Phillips
Editorial Board: Russell B. Adams Jr., Dale M.
Brown, Roberta Conlan, Thomas H.
Flaherty, Lee Hassig, Donia Ann Steele,
Rosalind Stubenberg, Kit van Tulleken,
Henry Woodhead
Director of Photography and Research: John
Conrad Weiser

EUROPEAN EDITOR: Kit van Tulleken
Assistant European Editor: Gillian Moore
Design Director: Ed Skyner
Chief of Research: Vanessa Kramer
Chief Sub-Editor: Ilse Gray

PRESIDENT: Christopher T. Linen
Chief Operating Officer: John M. Fahey Jr.
Senior Vice Presidents: James L. Mercer,
Leopoldo Toralballa
Vice Presidents: Stephen L. Bair, Ralph J.
Cuomo, Terence J. Furlong, Neal Goff,
Stephen L. Goldstein, Juanita T. James,
Hallett Johnson III, Robert H. Smith,
Paul R. Stewart
Director of Production Services: Robert
J. Passantino

THE ENCHANTED WORLD

SERIES DIRECTOR: Ellen Galford
Picture Editor: Mark Karras
Designer: Mary Staples
Series Secretary: Eugénie Romer

Editorial Staff for *Tales of Terror*
Deputy Editor: Tony Allan
Writer/Researcher: Ellen Dupont
Researcher: Peggy Tout
Sub-Editor: Frances Dixon
Design Assistant: Julie Busby

Editorial Production
Coordinator: Maureen Kelly
Assistant: Deborah Fulham
Editorial Department: Theresa John,
Debra Lelliott

Correspondents: Elisabeth Kraemer-Singh
(Bonn); Maria Vincenza Aloisi (Paris);
Ann Natanson (Rome).

Chief Series Consultant

Tristram Potter Coffin, Professor of
English at the University of Pennsylva-
nia, is a leading authority on folklore.
He is the author or editor of numerous
books and more than one hundred arti-
cles. His best-known works are *The Brit-
ish Traditional Ballad in North America, The
Old Ball Game, The Book of Christmas Folklore* and *The Female Hero.*

This volume is one of a series that is based
on myths, legends and folk tales.

Other Publications:

FIX IT YOURSELF
FITNESS, HEALTH & NUTRITION
SUCCESSFUL PARENTING
HEALTHY HOME COOKING
UNDERSTANDING COMPUTERS
LIBRARY OF NATIONS
THE KODAK LIBRARY OF CREATIVE PHOTOGRAPHY
GREAT MEALS IN MINUTES
THE CIVIL WAR
PLANET EARTH
COLLECTOR'S LIBRARY OF THE CIVIL WAR
THE EPIC OF FLIGHT
THE GOOD COOK
WORLD WAR II
HOME REPAIR AND IMPROVEMENT
THE OLD WEST

For information on and a full description
of any of the Time-Life Books series listed
above, please write:
Reader Information
Time-Life Books
541 North Fairbanks Court
Chicago, Illinois 60611

Library of Congress Cataloguing in
Publication Data
Tales of terror.
   (The Enchanted world)
   Bibliography: p.
   1. Horror tales. [1. Horror stories.
2. Folklore]
I. Time-Life Books   II. Series
GR73.T35 1987   398.2'5   87-1906
ISBN 0-8094-5277-4
ISBN 0-8094-5278-2 (lib. bdg.)

Time-Life Books Inc. offers a wide range of
fine recordings, including a *Rock 'n' Roll
Era* series. For subscription information,
call 1-800-445-TIME, or write TIME-LIFE
MUSIC, Time & Life Building, Chicago,
Illinois 60611.